Whose dark or troubled mind will you step into next? Detective or assassin, victim or accomplice? Can you tell reality from delusion, truth from deception, when you're spinning in the whirl of a thriller or trapped in the grip of an unsolvable mystery? You can't trust your senses and you can't trust anyone: you're in the hands of the undisputed masters of crime fiction.

Writers of some of the greatest thrillers and mysteries on earth, who inspired those who followed. Writers whose talents range far and wide—a mathematics genius, a cultural icon, a master of enigma, a legendary dream team. Their books are found on shelves in houses throughout their home countries—from Asia to Europe, and everywhere in between. Timeless books that have been devoured, adored and handed down through the decades. Iconic books that have inspired films, and demand to be read and read again.

So step inside a dizzying world of criminal masterminds with **Pushkin Vertigo**. The only trouble you might have is leaving them behind.

PUSHKIN VERTIGO

AUGUSTO DE ANGELIS

THE MURDERED BANKER

Pushkin Vertigo
71–75 Shelton Street
London, WC2H 9JQ

First published in Italian as *Il banchiere
assassinato* by Aurora in 1935

Translation © Jill Foulston, 2016

First published by Pushkin Vertigo in 2016

0 0 1

ISBN 978 1 782271 70 3

Text designed and typeset by Tetragon, London
Printed and bound by CPI Group
(UK) Ltd, Croydon CR0 4YY

www.pushkinpress.com

CONTENTS

1 · Fog   7

2 · Via Monforte… fort—   19

3 · The First Inquiries   33

4 · Shocking Evidence   47

5 · The Young Blond Man in the Attic   57

6 · "I don't know! I don't know anything!"   69

7 · Count Marchionni   83

8 · The Two Revolvers   97

9 · I Killed Him!   111

10 · A Great Love   123

11 · Pain Beyond Pain   133

12 · Darkness   147

13 · Trial and Error   161

14 · A Meeting with De Vincenzi   173

Epilogue   183

1

Fog

Piazza San Fedele was a bituminous lake of fog penetrated only by the rosy haloes of arched street lamps.

With a muffled sound of the horn, the last car moved slowly away from the pavement outside the Manzoni Theatre. The theatre closed its great black doors.

Ghostlike shadows were moving across the piazza. Two of them collided at the opening of via Agnello and one noticed that the other was that of a gentleman in evening dress, fur coat and top hat. For his part, the gentleman saw nothing but a black shadow. In any case, he wasn't looking. He was walking. From the piazza he proceeded slowly through the fog along via Agnello, continuing on his way.

As if he had recognized the gentleman he'd bumped into, the other man turned to follow him. But suddenly he stopped, uncertain, and drew out his watch. Bringing it to his eyes, he saw that it was some minutes past midnight. He hunched his shoulders and retraced his steps, hurrying towards the large door of the police station. He went in.

"So then, sir?"

"Ah. What do you want?"

"Anything?"

"Have you asked Masetti?"

"Why? Is the squad still working at this hour?"

"Masetti should be back... I sent him to Porta Ticinese. Go see what he's been up to."

"Petty theft, De Vincenzi. And he'll have found the fence's three bracelets." De Blasi's round, apoplectic face sneered. "That's his speciality, finding fenced bracelets."

"And what's yours, De Blasi? Abstinence?"

"I certainly wouldn't pretend to be someone who drinks water and lemon, like you."

De Vincenzi shrugged and smiled. He liked this journalist, round and red as a traffic signal at a blocked junction. Despite his florid drunkard's face, he was sharp and alert. Without a doubt, the best in the journalists' union, and it wasn't easy to put one over on him.

"Everyone has his weakness, De Blasi."

"Mine's not a weakness—it's a strength. Listen..." He entered the room and closed the door behind him.

De Vincenzi got up suddenly, hiding the book he was reading beneath a stack of files. "I've heard! Once you sit down, you'll be here till tomorrow morning and I already know your theories on the molecular properties of wine."

De Blasi remained unperturbed. He looked at the stove and grimaced. "Don't they ever change the stoves in here? That one over there is toxic. If you think I could put up with it... They've whitewashed the courtyard, changed the chief constable's furniture upstairs. Have you seen the red sofas? A bit hard, but at the moment there's not a speck of grease. And yet they don't change the old stoves or the faded old wallpaper for the rest of you, eh? Are you on night shift at the moment?"

"Look, De Blasi." The inspector, coming round the table, approached the journalist. "You're very agreeable company,

8

but for the next hour or so I need to be alone. Go off and find Masetti. Go to the Pilsen, go to the Galleria."

"In this fog and at three below zero? You're crazy!"

"No, it's warm at the Pilsen. And then you'll warm up quickly."

"You were reading?"

De Vincenzi pushed him towards the exit and as he did so, De Blasi pointed towards the stack of files on the table.

"You've buried your vice under crimes and misdemeanours! How many thieves and fences are heaped on top of Pirandello?"

"Get out of here! It's not Pirandello."

"OK, I'm going. But is it true that you study psychoanalysis? Ramperti told me. One of these days you must lend me Froind—is that how you say it? Who is Froind?"

"A gentleman who tries to excuse all your sins by saying that you dream them at night."

"Odd. But why did you become a policeman, De Vincenzi?"

"In order to have the pleasure of arresting you one of these days. Being drunk and disorderly is against the law."

"Hmph. When have *you* ever seen me drunk? Are you coming to the Pilsen later? Or maybe to the Cassé at four?"

"Yes, to the Cassé. Goodbye."

He closed the door, put a log in the stove and opened the damper. As for smoke… it did smoke, that stove. He looked around him. The night-duty room was squalid. On a table losing its veneer here and there, scorched by cigarettes and almost entirely covered by fliers, forms and files, the shiny new telephone seemed like a luxury item placed there by mistake. Or perhaps a surgical instrument.

He turned and sat down, took his book out from under the stack of paper.

It wasn't Freud. It was Lawrence. *The Plumed Serpent*. The senses...

He opened the drawer and felt for two other books: Plato's *Eros* and *The Epistles of St Paul*.

He leant back in his chair and looked at the ceiling. Why had he, after all, become Commissioner for Public Safety?

He jumped and shouted out nervously: "Come in", hurriedly closing the drawer.

"You! What are you doing here at this hour?"

Tall, thin, exceptionally elegant, wearing evening dress under his fur and a top hat on his head, Giannetto Aurigi came in quickly. He took off his hat and stood in front of the table, staring at De Vincenzi.

His eyes were shining, strangely bright, his face wan, gaunt and strained.

He smiled, and as he did so his thin lips disappeared so that his mouth looked like a slash.

De Vincenzi was struck by his pallor and red cheeks.

"Cold?"

"Fog! From Piazza della Scala you can't see the arched lamps of the Galleria. Needles in your face and your fingers numb with cold."

De Vincenzi looked at him with curiosity, interested.

"Inside La Scala, the Egyptian sun on the fans and the glory of the Pharaohs. And outside, the warden, stomping his feet."

He squashed the gibus he held in his hands. He looked around and went to put it down on a sort of bookshelf heaped with bound files.

He took off his fur and hung it up on a nail. Then, slowly rubbing his long white tapered hands, he went to sit down.

"And you came to San Fedele?!"

"Eh?" He was preoccupied and the question startled him.

"Well, yes. It's not the first time. I knew that you were on duty."

"I'm on duty every night here or there and it's a long time since you've come."

"You're right. But not because I'm not thinking about you. You're dear to me, you are. The dearest of all my classmates, even if—"

He stopped, as if slightly embarrassed, or maybe because his thoughts had changed direction. He laughed, looked around.

"It's depressing here."

"Police headquarters like any other. But you were saying: 'even if...' Even if I became a police functionary, right?"

"It must be a terrible life! Well! A natural inclination. There are thieves. That's natural too!"

"True." De Vincenzi mechanically touched the book in front of him. An unconscious reaction he didn't notice made him add: "Thieves and killers."

"What does that have to do with anything?" Aurigi's voice sounded shrill, almost false.

"I'm just saying. You're touchy tonight. *Aida*?"

The other man laughed. "Do you think it excites one's nerves? It's possible." He stretched out his long legs and rested his head on the back of the chair. His eyelids drooped.

De Vincenzi looked at him. Why in the world was he *here* at this hour? *And why had he come?*

They had been classmates and friends. They were certainly friendly, but not, perhaps, close. Come to think of it, where

11

could one find closeness these days, with men all hurling themselves towards their own destinies, with their own passions, their own needs and all the vices of the human body?

Each one of us has a secret, and the man with one he can admit to is fortunate.

What was Aurigi's secret? This man who, at nearly two in the morning, had felt the need to come and visit him, and who was now falling asleep there on the chair in front of him, as if he were worn out by fatigue or wakefulness or an unwholesome torpor?

The telephone on the table rang and the sleeping man started.

"What is it?"

De Vincenzi smiled. "Nothing. The telephone…" He took up the receiver and replied: "Hello?" He uttered some monosyllables and replaced the receiver. He looked at the other man. "You can go on sleeping."

"Sorry! Verdi's music…" He was clearly trying to pull himself together. He pointed. "That telephone there is going to be a torment, a nightmare for you."

De Vincenzi put his hand on the shiny black box, touching it almost lovingly. "My dear, tyrannical telephone! It's this which, during the long hours of waiting at night, connects me to the city… I'm exaggerating. Let's say to the world, my world as a policeman, head of the flying squad. Through it alarmed voices reach me, the first desperate pleas."

He smiled indulgently, as if sorry for himself. "For the most part, they are doormen awakened by the noise of burglars or the abrupt bang of a revolver or just by the din of a party of nocturnal troublemakers. Look at it! It's chunky, black, inexpressive. For you, nothing but a black box with a silly mouthpiece and a green cord. But for me it has a thousand voices, a thousand faces, a thousand expressions. When it rings, I already know whether it's bringing an ordinary administrative request or is about to announce some new drama, some tragic crime of passion."

Aurigi teased. "A mystery to crack!"

"Go ahead and mock. You're right. It's so rare, a mystery case. I'd like one! But I'm not looking for one and I don't expect one in the sense that you imagine: the detective mystery, the puzzle, a suspect to find and apprehend. No, no. Life is at one and the same time much simpler and much more complex. However, you see, there's always a mystery to excite me: tragic, deep... The mystery of the human soul."

"What a poet!"

Aurigi saw before him once again the friend of long ago. At school, too, he'd composed verses and recited them to himself, like someone possessed. "I was wondering..."

"Why I became a policeman? You're the second one to ask that tonight. But it's for that very reason that I became a policeman: because I am perhaps a poet, as you say. I feel the poetry of this profession of mine, the poetry of this dusty grey room, of this shabby old table, of the poor old stove, whose every joint suffers in order to keep me warm. And the poetry of the telephone! The poetry of the nights of waiting, with the fog in the piazza coming right up into the courtyard of this old convent—now home to the police station, housing criminals in place of saints! Of nights in which nothing and everything happens, because in this huge, sleeping city, even as we speak, there are infinite dramas, even if they're not all

13

bloody. Actually, the worst ones don't end in shooting or with a knife."

He stopped, as if a sudden idea had made him reflect. "Yes, a poet! You, for example, Giannetto."

Aurigi's shock was sudden and visible. "Me? What do you mean? What drama do you want to involve me in?"

"But no, who said anything about your drama? I was saying, Giannetto, you're a poet like me. Isn't it perhaps because of your love for poetry that you remembered your old school companion tonight and came here? In fact, why else would you have come, if not for that?"

"I've come lots of other times and you haven't made anything of it."

"True. But this evening is different."

"Are you investigating?"

De Vincenzi had a brainwave. "You need me tonight, Giannetto!"

"But of course! Aren't you the one, perhaps, who can explain it to me? At La Scala I was overcome by a strange lethargy. I fell asleep in my box. I was gradually overwhelmed by a sweet, unhealthy weariness. Then…"

"Were you alone?"

"In the box? No. It's the Marchionnis' box. Maria Giovanna was there with her mother. Marchionni came later. I was sleeping… a scandal. My father-in-law—my future father-in-law—pulled me into the foyer with him so he could lecture me. For days he's been looking for some excuse to do so. He says I'm gambling, that I spend my nights at the club, that I'm killing myself partying and that's why I fall asleep whenever I find myself with my fiancée. He spoke about big losses I may have incurred. He says that on the stock market, too, I've ended the month with a shocking loss."

"Is it true?"

"That I gamble? No."

"And on the stock exchange?"

Aurigi hesitated very briefly. He stared into De Vincenzi's eyes and shrugged.

"Oh, textiles have crashed."

"Did you have many?"

"Some. But that would if anything have been a good reason to stay awake! No, no. It's something else. I've told you: I feel all washed out. I left the theatre before the end of the third act. I needed to walk. The fog… the cold… the city, almost deserted. I made it to the Galleria and turned back. I came here to you. Am I boring you?"

"You're worrying me."

"You're joking, right? Don't start thinking that I have something unusual, something serious to reveal to you. That would be ridiculous."

De Vincenzi assumed the air of an innocent who asks lots of questions out of sheer curiosity. He smiled.

"What time does the third act of *Aida* finish?"

"I don't know, eleven… eleven-thirty… maybe later."

"And you were cold?"

"Me? Why?"

"You came here at half past one. Do the sums."

Aurigi shrugged.

All at once, De Vincenzi got up and went towards the calendar hanging on the wall. He put his finger on the red number and looked at Giannetto.

"Tomorrow is the 28th."

A look of terror went through Aurigi's eyes. The strength of his façade had crumbled and he suddenly seemed deflated. He murmured convulsively: "Eh, it's over."

De Vincenzi went to stand beside him.

"In it up to your neck, right? Like this?"

Giannetto's mouth contorted in a sinister smile.

"But you're joking, De Vincenzi! What are you trying to say? Simply that it's the end of the month… And I said so myself."

"So you did. The end of the month and of the accounts. Textiles?"

"They're coming back!"

"And you?"

"And me? I have steel."

"Which is falling."

"How do you know?"

"I see it written all over your face."

"Yes, it's falling. It's inexplicable, but that's how it is. I'm having a terrible time, De Vincenzi. You said: 'up to your neck'? It's worse, much worse."

He got up and took several steps across the poky room, moving like an automaton.

De Vincenzi watched him, unable to say at that moment whether he felt greater apprehension about the fate of his friend or a more cold-hearted desire to see him up to his neck in it and discover his hidden secret.

"Come on, you're a fine gambler! You have been since school. You'll get through this, you'll recover."

Aurigi then spoke hurriedly, as if to free himself by getting it all out.

"No, I can't sustain it. This time I can't take any more. It was already serious last month. I had to plunder all my resources. If I told you the sum you wouldn't believe it. This month I had to recoup and I risked everything. I dropped the textiles and bought steel… more than I could. Like a madman, or a clairvoyant, which is more or less the same thing. You won't understand."

"I understand you. Go on."

Aurigi stiffened.

"Why? Why are you making me speak?"

"Isn't that why you came here, to me?"

"To tell you about my ruin? You're mad! To what end? Can you give me a half a million? You? Ha ha!"

He laughed. It was clear that he couldn't keep from laughing at the idea.

"Can you give me half a million?" he repeated.

"No, obviously I can't give you that sum. But Count Marchionni…"

Giannetto stopped and looked at De Vincenzi, his eyes bulging, as if he didn't understand.

"Marchionni?"

"Naturally. Isn't he going to be your father-in-law? When are you getting married? Isn't he very rich, Marchionni?"

The other man violently shrugged his shoulders and started pacing again.

All at once he stopped.

"De Vincenzi, you've made me talk and I didn't want to. I came here in order not to think. Two hours, you said? OK—fine. But if you ask me where I went for two hours in the fog? I don't know. I walked. I suddenly found myself in the Galleria. And I came here, to see you."

"To the police station," De Vincenzi tossed out sarcastically.

"Yes, of course. To see you, not the station. It was a distraction. You might have had a good crime to tell me about. And a good crime, my man, would have been a way for me to stop thinking about my ruin."

De Vincenzi had barely had time to notice Aurigi's ominously dark tone and aspect when the black telephone on the table rang three times. Angry and lacerating, like three desperate screams.

2

Via Monforte... fort—

"Hello?"

De Vincenzi went to sit down at the table and took up the receiver. Aurigi turned his back to him and stared at the calendar.

"Yes, the flying squad… it's me… Hello, Maccari… Go ahead, tell me… No, wait." He picked up a pen and drew a pad of paper towards him from across the table.

"Go on, I'm writing… Good… Monforte… fort—"

De Vincenzi stopped speaking but continued writing in silence. With difficulty, he repressed a shudder. He shot a quick, terrified glance at Giannetto, who still had his back to him, before bending his head over a sheet of paper. For a moment it was as if a great space had opened up in his brain, but he instantly mastered his confusion and when he spoke again into the phone, his voice was calm and steady.

"OK… I've got the number… and the name, too. Is he dead? I understand. You'll wait for me, of course… I'll come immediately… I'll bring the officers I have here—but be ready to leave me some of yours. Goodbye."

He slowly put down the receiver. His look was harsh, his jaw tense.

"What is it?" Giannetto asked. He turned round and at the sight of his friend's face he repeated almost fearfully, "What's happened?"

"Nothing! Business, ordinary admin. So you wanted a good crime, eh?"

He pressed the bell button, still staring at Aurigi.

"Why was it tonight that you were wanting a good crime?"

"Me? But what's got into you, De Vincenzi?"

"Are you sure you were walking around for two hours?"

"But of course. I told you so. Why does it matter now?"

Short and stocky, with legs too short for his square, muscular body, Sergeant Cruni appeared at the door.

"You called for me, sir?"

"Yes. You and three other officers. A taxi. Right away!"

Cruni leant forward in a kind of bow that was both acknowledgement and leave-taking and made as if to go.

The inspector shouted after him: "Send Paoli in to me." Then he grabbed his overcoat and put it on.

"Are you going out?" Aurigi said. "I'll come with you."

"No. You can't. Wait for me here."

"Why do you want me to wait for you here? It's almost three. I'm going home."

However controlled he might be or resolved not to see in his childhood friend anything but a case that involved both his reason and his duty, De Vincenzi was visibly shaken. He repeated almost unconsciously, "Home? To your house?"

Aurigi looked at him, surprised. "Well, yes. Where would you like me to go?! But what's the matter with you, Carlo? Are you going mad?"

"Does it seem like that to you?"

He was about ready to arrest him and subject him to questioning: that might have been one way to proceed. But at once he decided against it and it was with a cold voice that he said:

"No, don't go away. Wait for me here. I implore you. I'll have something to tell you when I return."

The other man shrugged.

"As you wish. Why should I go home in fact?"

He smiled. Sat down.

Officer Paoli appeared at the door. "I'm here, sir."

De Vincenzi put on his hat, waved to Aurigi and hurried for the door. Paoli moved aside. The inspector whispered a brief order to him and left.

The officer was startled and now stared with professional curiosity at the man in evening dress who was sitting quietly, drumming his fingers on the inspector's table.

"Are you keeping me company?"

"If it doesn't disturb you." The officer's tone was neither sarcastic nor rude; it was, rather, obsequious.

"Bother me? Have a seat."

And he pushed an open cigarette case across the table towards him.

"Here are the others, God willing. That'll be it for tonight."

The bell rang. An officer got up from the armchair and slowly made for the door.

The drawing room was brightly lit. Too brightly. It was the kind of light you'd have at a reception, or for a surgical operation. The three doors were wide open: the one on the left, which led to another room, a small parlour; the one on the right for the dining room; and the one behind, which opened onto the entrance hall.

The other officer shrugged. "Well, it's better in here than at the police station."

Inspector Maccari appeared at the door to the drawing room: pudgy, round and full of bonhomie. He had his hands in his pockets, but his tense face betrayed a sense of horror, pity and anxious concentration, which contrasted strangely with the easygoing manner of a good bourgeois.

He stood at the door and looked straight through his officer. He was talking to himself, mumbling through his teeth.

"Well! An ugly crime… and anyone who understands the first thing about it is doing well! Why did this poor devil come and get himself killed just here?"

He noticed the officer sitting in front of him and looking at him, perplexed. He blinked, as if just waking up.

"Have you searched everywhere, you men?"

"Yes, sir, a first look round."

The officer got up and when he was next to Maccari he said dejectedly, "Anyway…"

"Anyway, they'll take it away from us, eh?"

"That's right. You called Inspector De Vincenzi, didn't you, sir? The flying squad… HQ will take on the investigation directly. It's a serious crime. They leave the break-ins and robberies to us."

The inspector twitched involuntarily, almost violently.

"And thank God, this time."

"Oh. For me… but does this crime really seem that opaque to you? The name on the door… the name in the deceased's pocket… the door wide open, no signs of a break-in… lights on…"

Maccari interrupted him good-humouredly. "Turned off, lad!"

"But no, sir. They were on, all of them just like now, that's how we found them, the entire apartment lit up like day."

"Right. And it was dark… Dark! The lights were on but it was dark, lad… and something wasn't right, something creepy in the dark, mark my words. It's not over. I'm telling you myself, this story has hardly begun."

De Vincenzi appeared at the door on the other side of the room. Behind him one could see the eager faces of the two officers he'd brought with him.

"Good evening, Maccari."

"Hello. Excuse me for having disturbed you, but I couldn't have done otherwise."

De Vincenzi looked around. He immediately fixed on the chandelier, which was all lit up, and he blinked in the glare, as he'd come from the fog in the streets.

"Imagine… and then… you don't yet realize what a good thing it was for you to call me… I'll tell you later."

He looked around once more.

"It was all like this?" he asked.

"Everything," the other man responded, and in his voice was a hint of condescendence. Maccari knew what his younger colleague would be looking for. Signs, clues, footprints, cigarette ash, the scent of the room… And for that matter, he wasn't laughing, either.

But he wanted to make things clear.

"As it happens, I arrived only a quarter of an hour ago. I looked around. I realized something wasn't right and I telephoned you immediately. You're young, with a career to forge. Me?" He smiled bitterly. "By this stage… And what's more, the dead bother me. I've seen more than one in my life… quite a few, perhaps, certainly too many for my nerves. What do you want? I can't stand the living. If I were bloodthirsty, I'd kill,

23

I would! But a man... a body fills me with pity, terrifies me."
He shuddered and turned to look around, as if to change the
course of his thoughts.

"Yes, everything as it was when we came in. The telephone
is there at the entrance. You'll have seen it... I telephoned
emergency to send a doctor. But there was only one of them,
and he had to alert his colleague at home. He'll come when he
comes. The man's dead; he can wait. Would you like to see him?"

Out of professional habit De Vincenzi had left his hat on.
The house wasn't a private place just then; it was a crime scene.
So he stayed in the middle of the room, his hands in the pockets
of his overcoat. Yes, he'd have to see the deceased sooner or
later. But first he had something else to say to his colleague.

He did not hesitate, even if a slight trembling sharpened
his voice.

"Did you know, Maccari, that this is the apartment of
Giannetto Aurigi? And in one of those coincidences that
never cease to surprise me, so strong is my impression it's only
chance that guides us, Aurigi is my old friend, schoolmate, and
just this evening—"

He stopped. Why tell everything?

"It doesn't matter. What is important, however, is that precisely because Aurigi is my friend, it's all the more necessary
that I keep my nerve and avoid making errors right from the
start. I already sense that if something escapes me, I won't find
it again. It'll be better if I go slowly and cautiously."

He took off his hat, feeling warm now. He put it on the table
and sat down. "Fill me in."

Maccari had been staring at him as he listened, scrutinizing
him in the way fat, jolly people do, with half-closed eyes. He

seemed to be winking, though he wasn't smiling. But when he spoke, his words were veined with irony as a matter of course.

"Yes, I know, that too is one method, you young ones follow a method these days. But hold on… I've studied, myself, a bit late, but don't think I'm doing it to learn. I'm doing it in order to get a feel for how many errors I've made or avoided over the last thirty years, ignorant as I am."

"Dead bodies make you bitter, Maccari."

"No. Hang on… I myself was hoping to cite a rule for your method. Here it is…" And he enunciated as if he were reciting a verse he'd learnt by heart. "The value of a fact lies not in its rarity, but rather in how common it is, and before claiming to reveal what is invisible to the eyes, it's a good idea to work on revealing what is all too visible—and which, for that very reason, does not attract attention."

He'd sidled up to De Vincenzi, now turning the irony back on himself.

"Good, eh?"

"If only one could always do that. And so?"

"So, less than an hour ago, I received a phone call: 'Come quickly to 45 via Monforte… there's been a murder!' 'Who is phoning? Hello? Hello?' But I was cut off… with these private phones, one can't check where the call is from, you know. I was somewhat dubious. I confess that at first I thought it was a joke. Then I said to myself: if I walk over there and find nothing, there's less harm done than if there were someone dead and I didn't go. I got here and found the door partly open, the stair light on as it usually is all night in these grand houses, and not a soul… But the main door was partly open, right? That was when I realized that this was no joke. The porters' lodge bolted… the porters asleep. I go upstairs and as I pass the first landing, Fanti says to me: 'Do you smell that?' An odour, in fact, like gas, but it wasn't gas, it was gunpowder, cordite. However, they hadn't fired in the stairwell, because if they had I'd have found the whole place awake. On the second floor, two doors, one closed, the other open… this one here… and one could see the entrance hall lit up. On the door, the name of Giannetto Aurigi. I go in. In the entrance hall, not a thing, but all the lights on. We turn around. A closed door down there. The servant's room, evidently. Empty. The servant's blue-striped waistcoat and his trousers and jacket were all thrown on the bed. That area, as well as the entrance, the kitchen: empty. In there, the dining room: dark—the only dark area. And empty. Nobody here. There, another sitting room, and stretched out on the floor in front of the sofa, a dead man."

He'd spoken hurriedly, working himself up, and he stopped to catch his breath. De Vincenzi was listening to him, trying to follow his words and not think about the riot of sensations and sentiments stirring in him.

Maccari started up again. "A dead man. A bullet hole in his temple, a trickle of blood on his face. The man was in evening dress. I search him…"

He looked in his pockets and pulled out a small wallet in green Moroccan leather. He felt it a bit and then held it out to his colleague.

"Here it is. This is his wallet. Small because of his evening dress. Inside there are five hundred lire and seven or eight calling cards."

De Vincenzi took the green leather wallet and opened it. Without rushing. Without curiosity. A strange state of mind had taken hold of him, numbed him: he had to see, he wanted to see, and he hardly could—or, to be precise, he slowed his movements, as if he wanted to delay their effect.

"Mario Garlini!"

He found the calling cards first and read out the name. He shuddered.

"He's a stockbroker."

"He was, you mean. Now he's a dead person. Yes, just like that, he was a stockbroker. But he was also more. The Garlini Bank was his. They say his net worth is thirty or forty million."

Maccari shrugged and shook his head. Thirty or forty million: a lot! He'd never see that much. But this man would never see that amount again. When it came down to it, there wasn't any difference between them now. He lived without all those millions, and thus he didn't really live. The other man was dead and his millions were his no longer. Maccari was depressed that night, and he said to himself: *We're dead, both of us.*

But aloud he only said: "Bah! Now he can't use it any more."

For the sake of saying something, De Vincenzi asked a question, the simplest he could think of in order to get the investigation going.

"Any signs of a struggle?"

"None. Not even an overturned chair. He must have been shot while he was sitting. His body slid to the floor."

"The weapon?"

"Nothing. If they didn't hide it somewhere in the house, which seems to me unlikely, they've taken it away with them. That would explain the smell of gunpowder on the stairs and it would suggest that the person who shot fled as soon as he'd fired."

27

"And then?"

"And then… What do you mean? I immediately felt this was a serious matter, and not just because of the dead man's thirty or forty million. Something doesn't feel right about all this. Don't ask me what, because I don't know. It's only my impression. But it was so strong that after I phoned for the doctor, I immediately rang you. Hurry up with it! Since I can, I want to stay out of it."

De Vincenzi got up. He grumbled, trying to follow Maccari's logic: "Bah!" But he forced himself to shake off the numbness that had come over him and continued.

"Didn't you have the porters woken up? Didn't you ring at the apartment next door?"

"No. But you'll have seen: the door is being watched and there's an officer on the landing."

"I saw…"

He suddenly went deliberately towards the door on the left, the one that led to the parlour. He looked at the dead man, but it made no impression on him. Only he asked himself, as if resenting the dead man, *Why did he die?* It was, naturally, a question without an answer. But in a sense there was an answer and De Vincenzi formulated it to himself, turning towards his colleague to observe, "He was still young."

"Thirty-five, thirty-six. Young."

"Did you search him thoroughly?"

"No, we didn't want to move him. I was waiting for the doctor."

De Vincenzi turned to look around the parlour. The usual: a blue sofa and two armchairs; a table, a sideboard, some pictures, no photographs. At the end, facing them, was another door. He didn't want to cross the room right then.

"And that door?" he asked.

"The bedroom."

"Lights on?"

"Yes."

"The bed?"

"Made up. With the sheets turned down and the pyjamas laid out, ready. It's clear that he hadn't lain down."

"Is that the last room in the apartment?"

"No. Another door. It was closed. I just looked: the bathroom. It appeared empty to me."

Sergeant Cruni had remained at the door in the entrance hall with Officer Rossi. But they were watching and listening. At that moment, De Vincenzi felt himself being watched and he suddenly called out.

"Cruni!"

Gratified, the sergeant stepped forward.

"Go and look in the bathroom."

Cruni hurried over.

De Vincenzi turned to Maccari.

"The streets are wet outside because of the fog. Did you find any footprints?"

The other man pointed at the floor. "Can't you see for yourself? Not a thing! They came by car, one would gather."

Silence fell between the two men.

Maccari buttoned up his overcoat, preparing to go. De Vincenzi removed his. Too warm in that apartment: even the corpse in the room next door had not gone cold. The atmosphere was heavy, burnt. The air in the radiators was too hot— they weren't letting the steam out, just retaining it. It was dry. That was the feeling! It was a feeling of dryness De Vincenzi had in his mouth. Between the joints of his fingers, too, he had that sensation. He wanted to act. He would surely have continued to question Maccari if he hadn't heard the bell at that moment, and a voice at the entrance saying: "Open up! It's the doctor."

Maccari and De Vincenzi started.

"He made good time," Maccari observed. He wished the doctor had taken a few minutes longer since he didn't want to get caught up in the mechanics of the investigation.

The doctor appeared, practically running. He was young and thin, with glasses, his nose sharp as a beak. He looked as if he were still a student, someone who didn't eat every day. He was carrying a black bag under his arm. It must have been one of his first official calls. One of his first crimes. A cadaver to study. He was conscious of the importance of the matter—and of himself, too. He found himself face to face with the other two men and advanced with his hand extended.

"Good evening, gentlemen. Doctor Sigismondi, from emergency services on via Agnello."

The other two introduced themselves.

"You'll find him in there," De Vincenzi told him, pointing towards the door on the left. "He's dead. I'd ask you, doctor, to make a note of the exact position of the body... get one of the officers to help you. You, Rossi, make yourself useful to the doctor. And I'd also ask you, doctor, to undress him—taking care that nothing should fall out of his pockets—and to let me have his clothing. But first, examine him carefully. See if there's been a struggle, and how long ago he was killed."

The doctor, not wanting to seem wet behind the ears, answered as if explaining something to him.

"Approximately, you mean. No one can establish precisely

when a man has died. Actually, one could determine it, but only with the right tools and taking the surrounding temperature… and these things are lacking."

Meanwhile, he'd removed his hat and overcoat and had started for the door indicated to him when Cruni came back in looking satisfied.

In a strange voice, as if he wanted everyone to hear, he said, "Not a thing, sir! The bathroom is empty."

He looked around and went towards De Vincenzi, signalling that he had something to say.

"Tell me," said the inspector.

The sergeant spoke, his voice extremely quiet, almost muffled. "Look in there yourself, over there… the bathroom is a mess. You might say there'd been a struggle. And I found this on the floor."

De Vincenzi took the object Cruni was holding and looked at it carefully. A phial of perfume, gold, one of those pretty little things women put in their purses. Engraved all over. He took it between two fingers and held it up against the light so he could see through it. "Colourless," he muttered. He sniffed and turned abruptly. "Doctor!"

"What is it?"

"Look here," and he held the phial out to him.

The doctor observed it, removed the stopper and brought it to his nose. "Bitter almonds! Where did you find it? Strange!"

"What do you mean, strange?"

"To have found this phial somewhere other than in its natural place!"

"And according to you, where would that be… the natural place for this phial?"

"A hospital or a chemist's. I don't think I'm mistaken when I tell you that it contains prussic acid."

The young doctor continued to look at the phial.

Maccari and De Vincenzi were quiet. They both felt a shiver run down their backs.

The dead man had been killed by a shot from a revolver. So what was the prussic acid doing there?

3

The First Inquiries

All three of them stood staring at the golden phial the doctor held in his hand.

The first to speak was the young doctor, who saw in this another way to enhance his role.

"In any case," he said, putting the phial in his pocket, "I'll let you know exactly what it is by tomorrow morning."

"Thank you."

But De Vincenzi needed to collect his thoughts for a few more minutes, to concentrate. To take note, chiefly, of his own state of mind, since he felt that his mind was not yet clear, nor his mood calm. He had the impression that all these facts and even the physical objects around him were escaping him and disappearing. And as they vanished, they began a crazy dance, a sort of witches' Sabbath.

"Doctor, will you take a look in there now?"

His tone was icy. Even the doctor looked at him, surprised. But he nodded and hurried into the parlour.

Cruni took hold of the inspector's sleeve.

"Go in there yourself, sir!" he mumbled, his tone almost pleading, so strong was his desire that his boss should see what he'd seen, and draw the conclusions that had escaped him.

After a brief hesitation, De Vincenzi made up his mind, and the two men followed the doctor.

Maccari stayed back on his own. He was thinking. And as usual, his thoughts came to his lips in the form of words. But he only spoke to himself.

"I said so! As far as I'm concerned we're only at the beginning…"

He felt defeated. A great weariness came over him and he sat down.

"Tomorrow morning, I'll say to my wife once more: 'My dear, only three more years, three long years… and then my pension! Retirement!' And she'll shuffle round the house in her slippers, grumbling: 'Great, your pension… for all that they'll give you!'"

But his thoughts were constantly shifting and they turned again to the incident he'd have liked to wipe from his mind for ever.

"The smell of gunpowder… a door half open… no sign of a break-in… a body. My pension! And the studies on method… the method! The description of the suspect… the significant facts. And all those people who steal and kill without even knowing the consequences. If only I didn't have to bother with it all."

He was startled when Sergeant Cruni ran back into the room.

"The telephone… where's the telephone?"

Maccari looked up at him. A few seconds went by before he answered, because he couldn't think what those words meant.

"Oh! Yes there it is, to the right, in the entrance hallway."

Cruni ran to it and grabbed the receiver. Within a few moments he was speaking with the inspector on duty at the station, telling him that De Vincenzi was on via Monforte at Signor Aurigi's house where there was a dead man, and that the dead man was the banker Garlini. At the other end of the line, the inspector on night duty listened distractedly, taking notes. Finally, with the air of someone who wondered what purpose was served by recounting all these things to him if his colleague De Vincenzi was there on the spot, he asked, "And so?"

But Cruni wasn't finished.

"De Vincenzi says you'll find Giannetto Aurigi in his office right now. He left him there himself and asked Officer Paoli not to let him go. Now the inspector asks that someone accompany him here right away. Listen, sir, the inspector says to send him here with two officers... no, no... without handcuffs... the officers should actually pretend that there's nothing the matter, and not say a word to him about the body."

Maccari had been listening from the other room. When Cruni returned, he asked, "Giannetto Aurigi is at the station?"

"Yes! Talk about strange, eh, sir?"

The inspector turned just as De Vincenzi reappeared at the door wearing an ironic smile. "He wanted a nice crime!" he exclaimed.

But all at once, as if to erase the sound of that sentence, he asked Maccari brusquely, "Do you feel there's a mystery here?"

"Me? No. I sense something worse: a tragedy."

"Why do you say tragedy?" De Vincenzi asked, looking him straight in the eyes.

"You'll see!"

For his part, De Vincenzi had the same impression. In that room, in that apartment, a heavy, gloomy atmosphere hung over everything like an invisible weight—something monstrous, inhuman. And not only the mystery of the body, but some other

35

unthinkable thing. *He felt it.* Not only was Aurigi mixed up in it—the friend with whom he'd studied at school and who was a poet like him—but everything, all of it felt strange.

"And you had Aurigi with you at the station?"

The question brought De Vincenzi back to reality. He smiled.

What a coincidence!

"He's your friend, you said?"

De Vincenzi was once more lost in thought. He muttered, "Leave it! It's terrible…"

As if to shake off the torpor threatening to overcome him, he suddenly turned towards the sergeant.

"Wake up the porters at once and bring them to me here! Have you phoned San Fedele?"

"Yes, sir. I'll bring them here right away. Inspector Boggi, who's standing in for you tonight, says he'll take care of phoning the chief constable."

As he went out of the back door, the sergeant failed to hear the inspector grumbling, "The police inspector, pah! We'll talk about that tomorrow morning."

He had to act now; he wanted to hurry things up. He went to the door and called for the doctor, who was still bent over the body he'd laid out on the sofa. He turned, saw the inspector, glanced again at the dead man and then returned to the drawing room, slowly wiping one hand against the other, like someone drying his hands.

"You want to know how long he's been dead, right?" He shrugged and said quickly, "The first signs of rigor mortis have set in… it must be two hours… two and a half. Over to you."

"What about his clothes?"

"They're in there, I haven't searched them. But if you'll allow me, I'll continue." And without waiting for an answer, he went back to the parlour.

In the meantime, Maccari continued to look around, all the while buttoning up his overcoat, as if the gesture could help him decide to get going and get away from the scene.

All at once he saw something shiny near the sofa. He bent down to pick it up. De Vincenzi watched him.

Instead of showing De Vincenzi the object, Maccari held it in his fingers. He asked, "Did you find something over there?"

De Vincenzi mechanically pulled a piece of paper halfway out of his pocket, and then quickly put it back to hide it.

"Yes, something... just what I needed in order to confuse me even more. You?"

"Me? Look at this!" Maccari held out the shiny object his podgy fingers were toying with.

A tube of lipstick. One of those pretty little tubes women carry around in their bags.

De Vincenzi looked at it, but made no comment. At that moment Cruni arrived with the couple who served as porters.

A strange couple: she young, quite pretty and buxom. And she was obviously afraid, but it was equally clear that a quiet irritation was troubling her generous bosom. He was a puny thing, rather gaunt, timid and completely terrified.

The woman spoke right away, without pause, approaching De Vincenzi as if she understood that he was the one she needed to address.

"What's wrong? A theft, eh? If something's been stolen, I can tell you myself who the thief is... I expected it. And it's his fault… that idiot's… because he should never have rented out the attic! But he has a kind heart."

She pointed to indicate her husband, who had started trembling and stuttering: "Rosa! Rosetta! What are you saying? Wait before you speak… you don't know anything yet!"

Suddenly full of unexpected energy, the runt turned towards the two policemen who were staring at him.

"Is it true, gentlemen? We don't know anything yet! Why did you wake us up? What's going on? Absolutely nothing!"

De Vincenzi had recovered his sang-froid. He'd gone back to being Commissioner for Public Safety and even his tone of voice had changed, become almost common—however unlike him that might be, proper gentleman that he was.

"You were sleeping, eh? The usual story. But shut up now."

He turned to the man with a hunch that he would speak more freely, while the woman would give him the run-around.

"Come here, you, and answer my questions."

The porter took a step forward, but his wife grabbed him and drew him aside with such violence that he teetered.

"Me, me! Ask me! What do you think *he* knows? During the day he's in the town hall. He works… he earns three hundred and seventy-five lire a month! Big deal! He really doesn't know how to do anything. At night he eats and then goes to bed! What do you think he knows?"

"And you on the other hand?"

"I spend the entire day in the lodge. I know everyone. I'm on my feet every evening until midnight. I close the main door at eleven; but it takes me a long time to get to bed."

De Vincenzi turned to Maccari. "Do you know them?"

38

"Never seen them. Have you ever been to the police station, you two?"

The woman protested indignantly. "Never! Oh! What do you mean!?"

The inspector shrugged his shoulders. "Me? Nothing."

De Vincenzi looked questioningly at Cruni and the two officers, but they too shook their heads.

"Good," he exclaimed. "So come here, little lady. Answer only when I ask you a question, and not so much chatter. Understood?"

"As long as you ask me things I know!"

Before continuing, the inspector turned to the sergeant.

"Go downstairs, Cruni. When they arrive from San Fedele with… that man, stop them and have him go into the lodge. I'll call for him."

Cruni disappeared again through the doorway and De Vincenzi turned back to the woman. She was curious, following his every movement, a faintly sarcastic smile on her lips.

"So… what time did you close the main door last night?"

"At eleven. What time should I have closed it?"

"You were in the lodge all day and throughout the evening?"

"Oh! What a question! Where should I have been?"

"Think hard before answering me: did you see Signor Aurigi during the day?"

The woman shrugged. "Yes, naturally, he was going in and out."

"What time? Give me the times when you saw him. Think carefully."

The woman's face was hard to read.

"How should I know? So many people go by during the day!

He must have gone out and come back at the usual times… in the morning at eleven—he never goes out before then. Then he comes back at one… he goes out in the afternoon. Wait. Today he must have gone out around three-forty-five. I know because he asked me if someone had come to look for him and I was ironing just then… and a short time later it was four, because I stopped ironing. I know it was four because I looked at the clock. At four-thirty the administrator was supposed to come and I wanted him to find everything in order. Not that things are not always in order, but you know…"

The inspector interrupted her.

"Keep going!"

The woman started.

"Eh? What do you want?"

"Keep going!"

"But you're interrupting me! Then… then… for sure, I can tell you… I remember it… Signor Aurigi came back, it must have been five. He wasn't alone."

"Who was with him?"

"An older man, upright, very distinguished."

"Had you seen him before?"

"Never."

The response was categorical. The woman was undoubtedly sincere. For that matter, why shouldn't she be? As yet, she understood nothing about it.

"And did they leave?"

"He… that gentleman left late, by himself. We were eating, and my husband had come back. It must have been half past seven, maybe later."

"And Aurigi?"

"He went out too, at nine, perhaps before. He was dressed for the theatre. He was going to La Scala."

"How did you know?"

"Where would he be going? It's hardly carnival time, when one goes to the balls! And then, he's always going to La Scala."

"Go on!"

"Go on... go on... I have nothing else to say. I didn't see him any more."

"You went to bed at midnight?"

"Wait... I'll tell you."

The woman paused. But her embarrassment appeared at once.

"Look. Last night I went to bed earlier. Right after I closed the door. I didn't feel well... neuralgia, I suffer from neuralgia."

"Fine."

"What do you mean, fine!" the woman screamed.

De Vincenzi shrugged. With all her chattering, the woman had served to help him pull himself together, but she was irritating him.

"Does Aurigi have a servant?"

She had to think about that question; it hadn't yet occurred to her. She looked around, as if for the answer.

"Well, yes. Isn't he here? Didn't you find him at home?"

Maccari and De Vincenzi looked at one another. Maccari drew up his shoulders. It could be a clue: a person who should have been there wasn't. Instead of the servant they'd found a dead man in the house. But both of them felt that it wasn't the right thread. It would have been too simple—a common crime, a thug's crime. And it wasn't like that. There was something behind it. Something worse.

41

"No. We haven't found him. Did you see him go out?"

"No, but it's funny. Giacomo never goes out."

"His name is Giacomo?"

"Yes. Giacomo Macchi. I know because he gets a letter every week."

"Is he old?"

"Well… he must be fifty. How should I know? He's an older man. He's grey."

De Vincenzi began again to question her about what particularly interested him.

"Aurigi… does Signor Aurigi receive ladies at home?"

The woman reacted with defiance rather than surprise.

"Ladies? Why would I know that? What does it have to do with the break-in?"

"Who told you there'd been a break-in?"

"Oh! What was it, then? Why are you here? What's happened?"

"Didn't you hear any noise in the night after one? The main door opening and closing? Anything unusual or suspicious?"

No, she hadn't heard a thing. And there couldn't be any doubt about it: she wasn't lying. She was still too surprised and too curious to think of anything besides discovering what was going on. If for no other reason, she was telling the truth.

All at once, De Vincenzi turned towards her husband. Grabbing his jacket and staring into his eyes, he asked, "And you! You heard nothing?"

The poor man shook like a leaf.

"Me? Ah! No, nothing."

His wife sneered. "Him? He just sleeps! If the palazzo were to fall down, he wouldn't even hear it." She looked at him with sarcasm and contempt. "He's always sleeping."

De Vincenzi felt sorry for the poor man. He'd have liked to shut the woman up right away, confront her with something that would terrify her.

"Are you feeling brave, little lady? As courageous as you are talkative?"

"What are you saying? What does courage have to do with sleeping?"

"Ah, you'll see, and then it will be difficult to get to sleep."

He pointed towards the door of the parlour.

"Look in there."

Instead of going towards the door, the porter's wife retreated. She became wary and looked around, as if she suspected a trap.

"In there? What's in there?"

The inspector took her by the arm and led her into the parlour.

"Come with me, and don't be afraid. In any case, being afraid won't get you anywhere."

As soon as they walked in, the porter's wife saw the doctor bent over the sofa. She didn't realize what he was hiding. She went forward, still cocksure, despite her increasing wariness. The doctor stood up and moved aside. The woman saw what was there and emitted a frantic scream—the scream of an injured beast. She tried to run, but De Vincenzi blocked her way.

"Oh, Madonna!"

"Come now. Be brave. Try to be brave and look at him carefully. Tell me if you've ever seen him, if you recognize him."

"No! Don't make me look at him. Madonna! Oh! How can I do it?"

The inspector's voice was chilly. Severe.

"I'm telling you to look at him."

43

"Oh, Madonna!"

The terrified woman turned to look at the dead man. She covered her face with her hands and would have collapsed had De Vincenzi not been ready to catch her and sit her down in an armchair.

He studied her. Why had she reacted so strongly? There wasn't anything that horrible about the dead man. A hole in his temple. Nothing else. Not even any blood on his cheek—the doctor had washed it away.

The doctor took a step forward. He felt it his duty to intervene since the woman was very unwell. But De Vincenzi stopped him.

"Let her be," he whispered. "Wait for a few minutes while she does what she wants. I want to watch her reactions."

Silence fell over the room. The porter's wife kept her face in her hands. She was drooping, her chest heaving.

Meanwhile, in the other room her husband had approached Maccari.

"Sir… Signor Commendatore…"

The inspector did not so much as smile.

"What do you want? Do I actually seem like a *commendatore* to you?"

The other man didn't understand the irony in the question.

"Tell me, *commendatore*, what's in there? What's happened?"

"There's a dead body. What's happened is that a man's been killed."

A tremor convulsed the little man. He clutched at Maccari's arm, his terror rendering him pitiful.

"Oh, my God! This house is cursed! Do they know that this house is cursed?"

"C'mon! Keep off me. What does the house have to do with anything? Men are sometimes cursed, but not houses! C'mon!"

The porter tried to stay upright and whispered, "Don't believe her, OK? It's not true! It's not true! If she says it was him, the tenant in the attic, don't believe her! He's a good lad. Poor but honest. I know it! Don't believe her." And he looked at the door of the parlour, fearing his wife's reappearance.

Maccari shrugged. "Tell that to the other inspector. He's the one making enquiries."

De Vincenzi came back in supporting the porter's wife on his arm. He had her sit down and then stood in front of her, looking straight into her eyes.

The woman watched him, her own eyes full of bewilderment and fear.

The inspector put his hands on her shoulders. "Now, talk!"

4

Shocking Evidence

A leaden silence descended on the men in that room.

The clock counted the minutes with audible clicks, like the ticking of a beating heart. The only one—all the others had stopped.

When De Vincenzi spoke, his voice betrayed the turmoil even he was feeling.

"Now you can't *not* tell me the truth. Did you know the dead man?"

The porter's wife seemed hypnotized by the inspector's gaze. She nodded "yes" mechanically, almost woodenly.

"Did he come to see Aurigi?"

"Yes."

"Often?"

"Every day for two or three days."

"And before that?"

"No, I don't think so… maybe, rarely. I've only seen him once or twice in all."

"And a woman came here to Aurigi's as well, is that right?"

The woman's eyes flashed with fear rather than surprise.

"How did you know?"

"Did she come often?"

"Yes."

"Every day?"

"Almost every day… but she stayed only a short time. It's not what you think."

"I don't think anything. And today? Did she come today?"

"Yes."

"And why didn't you tell me so?"

"I didn't know! I didn't think it was important. I was thinking about a break-in. The gentleman… Signor Aurigi didn't want me to let on that that… signorina came to visit him. He'd asked me not to tell anyone."

"He paid you well to keep quiet, didn't he? But that doesn't matter. What time did she come today?"

"At four. Shortly after Signor Aurigi went out."

"And she came up anyway?"

"Yes… she always went up without asking anyone. Today I would have told her; but then I thought maybe she knew that Signor Aurigi wasn't there."

"And how long did she stay?"

"I don't know."

"So, you're saying that when Aurigi came back this afternoon with the elderly gentleman the signorina was already in the house, right here?"

"Yes. She must have been."

"And you didn't see her leave?"

"After half an hour. She went by in a hurry, almost running. She was really pale. It made an impression on me so I went out to the pavement where I saw her get a taxi… in front, here… on the corner of via Conservatorio."

De Vincenzi turned round to Maccari.

"Would you be so kind as to trace that cab in the morning. If you find it, send the driver to me at the station."

Maccari nodded. He had listened to the whole interrogation and said to himself that De Vincenzi must know more than he was letting on, and must already have his own ideas about the signorina and the elderly gentleman.

De Vincenzi offered the porter's wife his arm and helped her up.

"Enough! Enough for now. Go back to bed, both of you, and keep quiet, eh? Don't speak to anyone about this, not even tomorrow, or I'll shut you up in the cells and keep you there. Off with you!"

He pushed the porter—still trembling and so small and stooped as to seem old and decrepit, and his wife, who by this time had lost her bravado—towards the door on the other side of the room.

He then took one of his officers aside and whispered: "Go downstairs with them and make sure they go to bed. See that they don't talk to Aurigi, who'll be in the lodge… that they don't say a thing to him, not a single word. Understood?"

"Yes, sir."

And the officer hurried to follow the porters as they left.

De Vincenzi and Maccari found themselves alone again. Cruni had gone to the entrance hall. De Vincenzi's brain was whirling. He was obviously struggling to stay on top of things and to see them clearly and precisely. He was trying not to think about Aurigi just yet. However, he was the actual cause of De Vincenzi's state of mind, one the inspector had never experienced before. A crime! Despite his youth, a crime would not really have upset him.

"You can't trust appearances," Maccari said, looking at him and shaking his head. "I have a feeling there's something behind this that's escaping us at the moment. Something horrible and unnatural. Too awful to contemplate."

The other man's exclamation was spontaneous, almost violent.

"God willing, if it were only unnatural!"

"Are you a friend of his?"

"Yes—and I thought I knew him."

"You thought him incapable of it?"

"Of killing? Of course. I didn't want to say so. I was thinking about something else… but I don't believe anything yet. You put it well: there are things that don't bear thinking about."

"Yes… the poison, above all. I don't understand the poison. Because, look—"

But he immediately interrupted himself, for the doctor was coming in from the parlour with the air of someone pleased to have accomplished something not only difficult but also interesting.

"I've removed his clothes; they're in there. I left the body undressed but covered it with a sheet. I can tell you that there was no struggle. One could say he was shot unexpectedly. The bullet entered the temple from the right, a little behind it, and stopped in the cranium. Tomorrow it can be extracted and then we'll see what calibre it is. But it must be a fairly large one, more than six millimetres. Death was instantaneous."

He put on his overcoat as he spoke. He then grabbed his hat and tucked his black bag, now closed up again, under his arm.

"I'll let you have a report on the poison tomorrow morning. Oh! I made a chalk outline of the body on the floor where it was lying. Everyone does it these days, in Germany, in America… Is there anything else you'd like to know?"

No, De Vincenzi didn't want to know anything else and he could have done without the chalk outline, even if they did it in Germany and America.

Before going off, the doctor repeated, "Naturally, tomorrow morning I'll be at the Monumentale cemetery at nine. Make sure the cadaver is on the table in the hall, and let the pathologists know I'm available. Goodnight."

"Thank you. Goodnight."

Maccari was so lost in thought that he didn't even reply.

They were alone once more. But De Vincenzi seemed not to be wavering this time. His glance had become hard and bright. He went towards his colleague and put a hand on his shoulder.

"Listen to me."

He fell silent, muttering to himself: "Yes, it's a risk, but I must run it. In the end, he's a friend, my childhood companion. I wouldn't do it for anyone else; but for him."

Then he raised his voice.

"Listen to me, Maccari. I'm asking you a favour, a big favour. It's true that I'll take responsibility for everything. But you're here now and tomorrow you could be asked to answer for it."

Maccari remained placid. De Vincenzi's preamble didn't really affect him. It was almost as if he'd been waiting for it.

"Oh. Go ahead, tell me."

"OK. Go downstairs. Aurigi is there. Go down as if you were the only one here. Tell him I left a while ago. Don't speak to him about… about what's in there… make up something for him, whatever you want—that there was a robbery in the house, that they didn't understand my phone call very well at San Fedele and they brought him here instead of just letting him know as I'd said to do. Try to give him the impression that

51

everything's over and it was nothing and... *get him to come up...
alone*. Understood?"

Maccari took it all in and looked at the inspector affection-
ately. He was young enough to be his son. He admired him,
even while telling himself that he might be doing something
very foolish.

"Have you thought it over carefully? It's a big risk."

"I've already said so!"

Maccari didn't hesitate. He shrugged. "You're young. You
can take some risks." For the umpteenth time he buttoned up
his overcoat and took his hat from a chair.

"Would you like me to stay down there?"

"No. Just ask Cruni to pretend to go off with the rest of you
but to turn back right away and stay in the porter's lodge and
wait."

"Right. Bye, and may God be with you."

Maccari left in a hurry. His greatest wish was to leave that
house, and even this final mission weighed on him. Oh! not
on account of the responsibility—he couldn't have cared less,
really—but he was frustrated by having to muster the energy
for it. He went downstairs with an officer in tow, pausing briefly
on every step.

Alone now, De Vincenzi went quickly into the parlour. He
looked over at the corpse. The doctor had covered it completely
with a sheet. He went nearer, without feeling any disgust, and
uncovered the face and a bit of the chest. The dead man now
had his eyes closed and seemed to be sleeping. Only the hole
in his temple was black, visible, and frightening.

He moved away unhurriedly and with some satisfaction. He
turned off the parlour lights.

52

In the drawing room once again, he looked around for a moment and turned off the lights there too. There were no lights on now apart from the ones in the entrance hall. He went in and dimmed them. The apartment was in total darkness, the dead man on the sofa.

De Vincenzi hid behind a cupboard in a corner near the kitchen. He felt his way through the shadows to the hiding place with some confidence—he'd spotted it beforehand.

He waited, barely breathing. He felt as if his thoughts were circling round a single point. And everything turned on this: *What will he do?*

He heard someone put a key in the lock, turn it, release the catch—and open the door. Giannetto appeared framed at the entrance, illuminated from behind by the lights from the stairs. His fur coat was open and he was still wearing his top hat. A bit pale, but not excessively so. He came in, closed the door and switched on the light. Looked around. He was clearly listening to the silence. He went into the drawing room and switched on the lights in there too. And there, too, he looked around, looked at the sofa, glanced at the closed door of the dining room and then at the open door of the parlour. He seemed almost surprised to find everything in order. All at once he stopped, shuddering as if he'd heard a step. He turned expectantly towards the door on the other side of the room. He didn't see anyone, and he grew more surprised. He drew a hand across his forehead. It seemed as if he were smiling, but his smile quickly vanished. He'd made up his mind, and he moved swiftly now, effortlessly. He went to the entrance, turned off the light and returned to the drawing room. When he reached the door to the parlour, he put his hand inside and adjusted the dimmer. He returned to turn off the light in the drawing room. And then with a sure step he crossed the threshold into the parlour.

A harrowing scream rang out.

As soon as he'd seen Aurigi turn out the drawing room light, De Vincenzi had emerged from his hiding place and walked towards the door. When he heard the scream, he quickly turned on the light, feeling as calm and confident as a surgeon before an operation.

Aurigi returned from the parlour. He'd taken off his hat and he was swaying. A crazed terror was written on his face.

De Vincenzi took several steps towards him.

Aurigi saw him. Desperately throwing out his hands, as if to escape from a terrifying shadow, he fell back into an armchair.

De Vincenzi continued in his direction, looking straight at him.

"You? Why?" Giannetto managed to utter in a strangled voice.

De Vincenzi answered him calmly, without a flicker, in the tone of someone wishing to reassure another. "Now try and pull yourself together. We'll talk later."

There was a fireplace on the left of the room. On the mantel-piece, a pendulum clock. The pendulum marked the hours: four loud strokes.

De Vincenzi jumped. He looked at the white clock face with its black points and then at Giannetto.

Aurigi had sat collapsed on the sofa for nearly an hour, as if concussed by a blow to the head. His eyes were open, but it wasn't clear that he could see. Nevertheless, he was looking around, perhaps at a shadow visible only to him.

De Vincenzi watched him for some time, telling himself that Aurigi's inertia could mean no good, and certainly wouldn't be productive. Inertia, which breeds confusion when it reaches the limit of human capacity. Because even the brain has precise limits and when thoughts go beyond them, they enter into a hazy, almost foggy region. It's craziness.

De Vincenzi sat down in an armchair by the table. He was trying on principle to keep out of Aurigi's line of vision so he could recover. But he realized that his friend not only wasn't recovering, but was lifeless and couldn't think rationally. He wanted to approach him, and he retreated almost fearfully.

In the next room, Sergeant Cruni and an officer were sleeping, perhaps on the sofa or perhaps not, since the sofa, which had been placed in front of the room containing the corpse, wouldn't have encouraged anyone to sleep.

Now that the pendulum had struck four, De Vincenzi deliberately got up and went into the adjoining room. He had to shake Cruni, who was sound asleep, to tell him: "I'm going home. I'm leaving Signor Aurigi to you; he's still here. Take care! You'll have to watch him, but not just because he might escape. Understood?"

Cruni nodded, now completely awake.

"I'll return tomorrow morning. They'll probably come to remove the body. If the investigating magistrate comes, tell him that I left the house at four and will return at nine."

He went back to the drawing room and glanced at Aurigi, who'd finally stirred. And he had moved more than a little. Even without seeing him, De Vincenzi could guess from his current position what had happened: he'd toppled onto the sofa in a sort of complete collapse and closed his eyes. He must have been feeling literally broken up.

De Vincenzi watched him only briefly. He wanted to be able to think beyond him, beyond the point of having a precise image in front of him. He'd seen him stretched out. That was enough. He didn't want to observe the contractions of his face, the deep creases that had formed around his mouth and on his smooth skin, the dark circles around his eyes.

He left in a hurry.

Cruni went into the room and looked at Aurigi, who seemed to be sleeping. Then he himself sat down in the armchair near the table, occupied earlier by the inspector. He had to wait for time to pass.

He looked at the clock and jumped to his feet. It said ten past five. The sergeant drew his own watch from his pocket and continued looking for several minutes at the two timepieces.

They should have been keeping the same time, but he saw beyond the shadow of a doubt that there was a huge difference between them.

5

The Young Blond Man in the Attic

Only a few hours of restless sleep. Now he'd bathed and was leaving. Though it wasn't yet eight, De Vincenzi felt like walking. He would go all the way to via Monforte on foot. He lived on Sempione, a long street. The morning was freezing-cold, with wispy fog that got gradually thicker higher up, as if it were rising towards the heavens from Sempione Park. One couldn't see the sky, except in the form of more fog above—thicker, greyer and deeper.

De Vincenzi didn't go across the park, which would have been the shortest route. He wanted to walk. When he'd got back home around five, he'd thrown his clothes on the bed and gone to sleep. A sleep full of nightmares. And now he felt the need to think with a clear head.

He knew Giannetto—or thought he knew him. Sometime poet of life, his wings clipped by necessity, by vice, by a boundless desire for enjoyment. Not, perhaps, of unbending morality, yet only in the sense that he'd never gone to the trouble of formulating for himself the rules of such a code. But honest? Yes. Certainly incapable of committing a crime, or of committing it in this way, which was both clever and stupid, clean and messy.

Because in fact the picture looked like this. Aurigi owed a sum of money to Garlini. A lot. A huge amount, perhaps. He couldn't repay it; he'd said so. In any case De Vincenzi knew that it was a fact which could easily be checked. According to his account, Aurigi had gone to La Scala but had left the theatre at eleven and then wandered around the city.

If one could rely on his word. However, De Vincenzi wasn't obliged to trust him without first having suspected him and evaluated the situation, and he had to admit that Aurigi could easily have committed the crime sometime between eleven and around one, when he'd shown up at San Fedele. But what had he done afterwards? Something that was both very clever and stupid. He'd come to him, De Vincenzi, at the station and had shown himself to be nervous and agitated. He had spoken in broken phrases, which could only indicate an unusual emotional state. Yet did that mean it was the state of a killer?

If he'd been able to behave differently, despite all the turmoil caused by his action, and to reason that it was better to come right here to the station... yes, it would have been clever for him to have found his way to De Vincenzi, to dispel serious suspicion. Or maybe he'd come here in his initial confusion without knowing what he was doing.

De Vincenzi remembered now. At midnight, on his way to San Fedele, he'd bumped into a man in evening dress and top hat. And that man had been Aurigi. He'd been coming from the piazza in via Agnello, walking without looking at anyone, passing through the cold of a winter night. He remembered now, with some surprise at not having thought of it before. When he'd seen Aurigi before him in his office in San Fedele, why hadn't he asked immediately: "I saw you an hour ago walking through the fog in front of this building. Where were you going?" And why had he not immediately connected that encounter with his friend's agitation?

Surely, he couldn't have foreseen that fifteen to thirty minutes later the telephone would announce that there was a body in Aurigi's house. All the same...

So, Giannetto *could* be the killer. He might soon discover the motive, if not actually the evidence. But De Vincenzi *sensed* that that wasn't the truth, that there was something else involved, both more obscure and more complicated.

If not Aurigi, then who?

The porter's wife had ended up admitting that a signorina went to Aurigi's almost every day. And that signorina, De Vincenzi guessed immediately, had to be his fiancée, Count Marchionni's daughter. What's more, an older gentleman had also gone to Giannetto's house that day and she must have met him—or maybe she'd decided not to see her fiancé, if only because there was a third person present.

The line of inquiry was more solid here, more direct, and De Vincenzi wanted to persuade himself that he should follow it. But how far? And where would it lead him?

At that moment an image of the pretty, buxom porter's wife and her scrawny little husband flashed before his eyes. He heard that pleading voice again:

"Don't believe her! Don't believe her!... We don't know a thing!"

And she, the woman, had immediately accused *that man in the attic*. "If there's been a break-in, he's your thief," she'd said.

Who was he?

He now regretted not having paid attention to that detail and getting right to the bottom of the matter. He would do so as soon as he got to via Monforte. But he had something else to do first.

Arriving in Piazza Cordusio, he noticed that he'd gone too far, lost in thought. He turned back and went up via Meravigli. It was easy to find the Garlini Bank: two large, shiny brass plaques on either side of the main doors.

He went in and saw the guard and some of the employees. Early birds—it wasn't yet nine. But the cashier was there. A big man: tall, fat and red in the face. A short neck on wide, square shoulders supported his heavy blond head.

An unfortunate build for a cashier! thought De Vincenzi. If he had a heart attack at the window he'd frighten the devil out of everyone… His irony had returned.

He questioned the man quickly. The cashier was anxious to tell De Vincenzi everything he knew. De Vincenzi took a look at the books, but stopped instantly: it was wasted effort, since he understood nothing. The expert accountants would be here before long and he would learn what he needed to know in any case. He listened to the cashier instead, and made him repeat something.

"You're sure of it?"

"I'd swear to it," exclaimed the other man, going redder still. "I took it from this bundle right in front of him in order to give it to him. See? There's eighty, not a hundred. Do you want to count it?"

No, the inspector did not want to count it. "What was it for?"

The cashier laughed in that way of his, a kind of forced snicker peculiar to the rubicund.

"Ha! If you think the boss would tell me his business! Look, maybe some chick… he liked his girls, you know?"

Another fact he'd have to take into consideration.

But right away he shrugged. Fast women in Aurigi's house!

He was increasingly focused on the case, completely immersed in it. He went into a cafe and drank two cups of coffee, one after the other. He looked at his watch and saw that it was already almost nine, so he hopped into a taxi which took him to via Monforte.

As he went past the porter's lodge, he saw the porter's wife watching him with bright, anxious eyes.

He went in. The woman could barely manage to say "Good morning", she was so anxious that he was about to say something.

The dead man in the building had shocked her. She hadn't even combed her hair, and without powder her face was shiny, like the sweaty face of a fat woman.

"Start talking!" De Vincenzi laid into her. He had no time or appetite for formalities. The porter's wife was startled.

"What's going on—more?"

"Last night you were talking about the attic… about a man who lives there who'd be capable of…"

She gulped.

"I said that… when I thought there'd been a break-in. But now!"

"So who is the man you were speaking about?"

"A young lad. A distinguished one, by all appearances. Though he can't have a penny. There was an empty room on the top floor. See? One of the rooms they give to servants… and my husband wanted to rent it to him. It must be two years ago by now. He stays up there almost all day. I think he writes or something… he says he's working on novels, short stories. But you can be sure his stories aren't putting chicken on the

61

table, because he got himself a little camp stove and in the morning he goes out to buy something."

"What's his name?"

"Remigio Altieri."

"On the top floor, you said?"

"Yes, he's on the same staircase as Signor Aurigi."

The inspector left the porter's lodge and climbed up to the fourth floor. As he went past Aurigi's apartment, he noticed the half-open door. He hurried by, not wanting to be stopped just then.

He found Altieri's door easily. It was the only closed one. All the others opened onto a long corridor lit by an electric light that was left on.

He knocked, and a young blond man dressed in black appeared at the door. He stared at his visitor in surprise.

"Signor Altieri?"

"I am he."

"Would you allow me…" De Vincenzi entered the room and walked past Altieri, who instinctively withdrew.

"I must speak to you."

He looked around. It was a humble room, but very clean, and the furniture was noteworthy. There wasn't much, but it was antique—what was left, perhaps, of a bygone prosperity. Or furniture parents had removed from a luxurious house in the country to give to a son who'd moved to the city.

A student, thought the inspector.

The young man remained near the still-open door, watching him. He was so bewildered that he was beyond irritation or offence at this almost violent intrusion. He simply accepted that he couldn't explain it.

De Vincenzi noticed a bed, a chest of drawers, a table with an armchair in front of it and, on the table itself, a large portrait of a woman.

A pretty woman: she must be young. A great mass of hair, two deep-set, luminous eyes.

The room was suffused with the scent of cigarettes and eau de Cologne.

Poverty? Misery? Scanty meals, sometimes missed? The inspector searched in vain for evidence of a fireplace or a gas burner. But as for misery, if it could be called misery, it had such a dignified aspect that it instilled respect, if anything.

"I'd like to put a few questions to you, Signor Altieri. I'm Commissioner for Public Safety."

The young man seemed unafraid. In fact, one might have said he was no longer surprised. However, he closed the door with great care and went towards De Vincenzi.

"I don't understand…"

"Naturally. How long have you been in Milan?"

"Two years."

"And before that?"

Altieri smiled. From his pocket he pulled out a piece of folded paper. He held it out to the inspector.

"I believe it will be quicker for you to read my identity card. I was born in Nancy."

"French?"

The young man nodded. "French."

"But how did you come to speak Italian so well? Without an accent?"

"Indeed! I've been in Italy for ten years. I was fifteen when I came here."

"On your own?"

"With my father."

"And now?"

"By myself. My father died nine years ago. One year after we found ourselves in Italy."

"And you?"

"It's quite a story!" exclaimed Altieri. "Do you really want to hear it? In that case, please sit down."

In answer, De Vincenzi sat in the armchair.

The young man went to the other side of the table and he too sat down, in the only chair.

"If you would tell me, Inspector, why you're interested in me, perhaps I might give you the explanations you need without offering you lots of useless information."

"I'd prefer to hear everything, even the useless things." De Vincenzi's tone was somewhat abrupt.

He regretted it at once. After all, the young man seemed *simpatico*. And he was obviously wasting his time. How could he consider that Altieri had killed Garlini, or that he somehow knew something about the tragedy?

The young man raised his eyebrows, once more surprised. "Right, if it makes you happy."

So he told the story of his own life simply, without expression and without working himself up. He did it as if it had nothing to do with him, and it was clear that by now he must be completely separated from his past, having made a clean break with it.

A few other things—quite deep and important—tied him to the present and to the future. And perhaps that very past was a dead weight, which distressed him.

"I was born in France of an Italian father and a French

mother. You can see that on my identity card. My mother was a duchess of Noailles. She eloped with my father and married him against the will of her family. My father was a painter who'd gone to France to try his luck. My mother eloped with him. Her parents never forgave her. She lived in poverty with my father. Dad had a lot of talent, but not much luck."

He paused, and then murmured: "Like me!" He blushed immediately and looked down.

De Vincenzi glanced at the photograph on the table. Altieri noticed, and seemed even more embarrassed.

"I meant like me as far as luck is concerned!"

He quickly resumed his story. His mother had died after fifteen years of marriage and his father had then returned to Italy with his son. He'd taken with him the furniture he'd had in Paris. The young man looked around. He'd sold much of it: this was all that was left.

Then his father, too, had died, leaving him alone. He'd studied, and had got by giving lessons in French. He'd been a tutor to a few wealthy families, but he didn't earn his living that way. He'd started to write of his own account. He was working for several publishing houses, doing translations.

That was it.

"And now, what can I help you with?" he asked, with such stark simplicity that it bordered on irony.

Clearly, he couldn't help him with anything. De Vincenzi felt he'd got lost in time: the tale—rather ordinary, to tell the truth, and a bit too much like a children's adventure story—had so interested him, and the tone of the narrator had been so genuinely calm and serene.

Apart from being resigned, he was irrelevant to the inquiry.

65

An intelligent young man, without a doubt. One could see that he was of good breeding. A duchess of Noailles! And his father a painter. Much talent, little luck. "Like me!" he'd involuntarily exclaimed.

That was true, after all.

Well, what else was there to do? De Vincenzi had to get up, express his thanks, excuse himself and go on his way.

"Forgive me for having disturbed you. I've questioned you as I did all the other residents in the house. A crime was committed here last night…"

The young man flinched.

"A crime?" he asked.

"Yes. A man was killed. The banker, Garlini. Did you know him?"

"No, I did not!" he answered.

But the inspector heard a slight trembling, some hesitation in his voice. So he added, looking Altieri in the eye: "He was killed in Giannetto Aurigi's apartment."

This time the young man leapt up so violently and unexpectedly that the table on which he was leaning wobbled. He went pale. As white as wax. And the pallor on his subtle, aristocratic features, gave him the look of an ill person.

"Do you know Signor Aurigi?"

"No," he mumbled.

He was lying. He was so obviously lying that he was afraid of his own lie and hurriedly blurted out, "I mean… I know his name… I've bumped into him a few times on the stairs…"

"Where were you last night?" De Vincenzi asked coldly.

The other man looked at him in surprise, uncomprehendingly.

"What did you say?"

"I said, where were you last night? From midnight until one."

"But here! In this room. Oh! Where do you think I was?"

"And you heard nothing?"

"Not a thing!"

"Were you sleeping?"

"No. I may have been writing. Or I may have been reading."

"And there's no one who can verify your alibi?"

"Alibi? Why do you say alibi?"

De Vincenzi smiled. Actually, he'd gone too far. Of course the boy was upset when he heard the name Giannetto Aurigi, but did that mean anything? Could one surmise and believe that he was the killer on that basis alone?

There had to be something hidden behind it; but to think that that boy had killed Garlini was too much. Why? It was true that twenty million lire were missing from the packet: *I counted it in front of him in order to give it to him*, the cashier had said.

But this man wasn't the type to commit a common crime or a break-in.

Unless… and De Vincenzi looked at the photograph on the table: a woman!

"Fine. We'll talk again. I'll come back here or send someone for you."

He left in a hurry.

The young man stood for some time looking at the door the inspector had just left through, whispering, "In Aurigi's apartment!"

He looked at the photograph, and his entire face lit up with tenderness. And terror.

6

"I don't know!
I don't know anything!"

De Vincenzi hurried down to the second floor.

He rang at Aurigi's door, which was now closed, and had to wait a moment or two before Cruni opened it. The sergeant was still sleepy.

Once again, the inspector entered the room he now knew so well; its every detail was impressed on his brain.

Aurigi was sleeping on the sofa, crumpled and exhausted. He was still in evening dress, his overcoat wrapped round him.

"Has he been sleeping the whole time?" De Vincenzi asked Cruni.

"Like that, just as you see him. Now and again I thought he was dead... him too! Then he would get restless and fidgety and utter meaningless half-sentences..."

"Did you write them down?" the inspector asked almost automatically; he was imagining the phrases the sleeping man might have uttered.

"They're over there." The sergeant pointed to the table. De Vincenzi saw a sheet of paper covered with notes. He looked at Cruni. He'd never have expected his underling to have demonstrated such intelligence.

"Read them. You'll see they won't be much help. They don't mean a thing."

De Vincenzi took the paper and read:

"No, don't do that! I'll pay! You must not get involved… A lot of peace, a little quiet time… I'll go away, yes, I'll go away…"

Meaningless? He would see him later, when he was refreshed. But he was fairly happy with the sergeant's observation, since it showed that his subordinate's intelligence only went so far after all. And in this case above all, he wanted to rely completely on himself. Anyone else's help would do nothing but derail him. If he wanted to reach his goal, he'd have to follow his own instincts, his own mysterious intuition. But what goal? He didn't want to admit to himself at that precise moment that his whole being— quite obsessively and unexpectedly attached to his schoolmate of so long ago—was pushing him to save his friend at any cost.

Every now and then his thoughts returned to the young man in the attic. He couldn't forget the boy's appearance. An interesting face, without a doubt. Even when it was pallid—in fact, even more then.

But why had he blanched at the name of Aurigi?

Without being able to explain why he was doing so, De Vincenzi began contrasting the two men. Two fine examples of humanity! Even if one was still practically a boy. But how mature he was, how conscious already of life and its sorrows. This one here was more of a man, albeit with a character less deep, less passionate, more superficial.

Until now, he'd known only life's pleasures, while the young man already knew all the bitterness of renunciation, sacrifice and struggle. But he'd come through the storms, while right now Aurigi appeared shaken, overwhelmed.

The other man, however, had experienced such a shock that he'd collided with the table.

De Vincenzi watched Giannetto sleeping. He realized he was still holding the sheet of paper Cruni had given him. He put it back in his jacket pocket before asking, "Did the investigating magistrate come?"

"Yes, at seven. He wanted to talk to you. I told him you'd been up until four. Because, sir, you left this house at four and not at five."

De Vincenzi looked at him. He moved away from the sofa where Giannetto was sleeping and, looking Cruni squarely in the eyes, he asked quietly, "Why does that matter? What are you trying to tell me?"

Cruni lowered his voice in turn. "I mean that this clock, here," and he pointed to the clock on the mantelpiece, "is one hour fast."

De Vincenzi took his watch from his pocket and looked at the clock with a jolt. But he said nothing and put the watch back.

"It doesn't mean anything. You were telling me about the investigating magistrate."

"He's coming back later."

"Who is it?"

"I don't know him. He's young. It seems, though, from what the registrar said, that the public prosecutor will see to this business personally."

The inspector shrugged. "Provided he leaves me some space to act…" He nodded towards the sleeping man. "Have you questioned him?"

"Yes. But he didn't say anything. His personal details, and

that was that. To every question he answered: 'I don't know anything'."

There was a silence. De Vincenzi looked around. He went to the door of the room and turned towards Cruni.

"They took the body away, yes?"

"Right after the investigating magistrate gave clearance."

"Did the investigating magistrate search the apartment?"

"Like so!" The other man waved his arm. "He looked around... said he'd send forensics to take samples... but he was smiling, as if to imply that all of it was pointless. I have the impression that he was convinced of the guilt of the man sleeping over there. He asked if you'd declared him under arrest."

This time, the inspector neither jumped nor smiled. Of course! He would have to declare him under arrest. But it would be pointless.

Silence fell once again. De Vincenzi moved towards the entrance hall, then stopped.

"The servant?"

"Nobody's seen him."

"Get Inspector Maccari on the telephone for me."

The sergeant looked at his superior in amazement.

"But he'll be sleeping, sir. He was on night duty."

"Call the Duomo police station. If Maccari isn't there, someone else will be."

Cruni went to the telephone. He soon appeared at the door, holding the receiver at the end of its long green cord.

"Here you are, sir."

De Vincenzi took the receiver. "Hello! Ah, it's you. Yes, good morning. Did Maccari leave the report for you? Good. Yes, the chief constable naturally entrusted the inquiry to me.

Look, I need you to find me the taxi driver right away, the one who drove the young Contessa Marchionni yesterday... Yes, he was at the stand in via Monforte on the corner of via del Conservatorio... at five or five-thirty... Yes, thanks... One more thing! HQ has given orders to look for the servant... Giacomo Macchi... They'll have telegraphed the description all over Italy and the borders... You should look for him too... Definitely let me know if something about him turns up... What? Nothing in the filing cabinet. Thanks... Nothing else for now... Ah! When Maccari arrives, please ask him to telephone me. Thank you. *Ciao!*"

He hung up and went back to the drawing room.

Giannetto Aurigi was still sleeping. He was no longer agitated; he wasn't even moving.

The inspector resumed his conversation with Cruni.

"Have you taken his next-door neighbour's details?"

"I asked Verri to do so and he brought me the owner's business card. He's an engineer."

"Do you have it?"

"What, the business card? Here it is. I had Verri leave it with me. He wanted to deliver it to you personally."

De Vincenzi took the card and read: Vittorio Serpi. He didn't know him. He asked, "Does he have family?"

"Wife... two kids... a maid."

"They heard nothing?"

"Nothing."

"What time did he come home last night?"

"At twelve. After the theatre. He says he found the door closed and the stairs deserted."

"And the smell of cordite on the stairs?"

"I don't think so. He would have said."

"Get him to come to the station later this afternoon… with the rest of his family."

A muffled groan rose from the sofa and the man stretched out on it moved. He wasn't raving. He was no longer immersed in a nightmare. He was slowly waking up, coming from the dark of night to the dawning of perception.

De Vincenzi grabbed Cruni's arm and pushed him towards the door on the other side.

"Keep quiet! Go over there… don't reveal yourself until I call you."

Cruni disappeared.

Giannetto shifted around on the sofa, still emitting little groans from time to time, as if he were trying to find a position comfortable enough to go back to sleep in. But he couldn't, and he opened his eyes. He looked around to see where he was. He saw the room with its familiar furniture and then inspected himself—still in evening dress, with his fur coat on. An expression of profound wonder spread over his face. He did not understand.

He glanced at De Vincenzi. A light flashed through his mind and he leapt to a sitting position on the sofa. His face was strained, taut and fixed.

Affecting indifference, De Vincenzi said jovially, "Good morning! Did you sleep?"

"I did." Giannetto answered in an almost toneless falsetto. He slowly rose.

"You slept on the sofa! It isn't the most comfortable spot…"

"I didn't have a choice—did you want me to go in there?"

74

But he didn't turn round to point at the door to the parlour. He was definitely still petrified.

De Vincenzi, however, stared at the door and answered nonchalantly, as if to show he thought nothing of it.

"Oh! You can go in there now. He's gone."

Giannetto interrupted him. His voice verged on the shrill. "I know."

"Were you awake when they took him away?"

"Yes."

He shivered visibly and turned in on himself.

A long silence followed. Too long. The inspector wanted to end it but couldn't find the right phrase. Finally he asked, "Did the investigating magistrate question you?"

It seemed as if Aurigi were waking up again, he'd been so absorbed.

"What were you saying? Yes. This morning…"

"And?"

"I did not confess."

The sarcasm in his reply was painful. It wasn't bitter; it was raw.

For De Vincenzi, it was time to get to the bottom of things. He shrugged and exclaimed with a policeman's brutality: "Well, it wasn't necessary, either."

Giannetto sneered. "Indeed! Who'll believe it wasn't me?"

"You weren't here?" De Vincenzi said immediately—almost hustling, he was studying Aurigi so intently.

"Oh, believe what you want—you, too. At this point."

His words revealed him to be so crestfallen, without any fight left in him, that his friend took him by the arm and forced him to stand up.

"Look at me, Giannetto! What's happened here is frightening, for you above all. I'm trying to believe in your innocence—I want to. I'll tell you something else: it's your friend speaking, the friend who was your schoolmate years ago. Believe me! I'll tell you what duty prohibits my telling you: there's something so grim about this, so paradoxical... so terribly clever that it makes me believe in your innocence. For the love of God, help me out. Speak! Tell me everything. Help me discover the truth, even if you're ignoring it."

The other man appeared unmoved. He seemed insensate. His shoulders fell again.

"At this point," he repeated.

De Vincenzi felt another jolt, and this time its force made him really brutal.

"But don't you understand, idiot, that you're risking your life? All the evidence is against you! Don't you understand that I can't do anything for you if you don't give me some way of discovering the truth?"

"I don't know! I don't know anything."

"Don't you realize, Giannetto, that no one can possibly believe you when you say you know nothing? This is your apartment... the lock wasn't forced. Do you understand what I'm saying? And then, how can anyone accept that Garlini entered your house to be killed *by someone else*, if you didn't bring him here? Garlini was your stockbroker, and while I'm standing here talking to you, the experts are examining the bank's books. They'll find the figures from your game, they'll say you'd have had to pay Garlini's bank almost half a million by tomorrow."

Giannetto was obviously listening to him, but he didn't move. His face was inscrutable.

The inspector shuddered, as if an idea had suddenly occurred to him.

Slowly, articulating his words with care, he asked, "Did you *really* have to pay half a million to Garlini?"

"What are you trying to say?"

De Vincenzi proceeded to speak so plainly and with such sincerity that Aurigi was momentarily really shaken.

"Listen to me, Giannetto! You know this: except in cases of insanity, committing a homicide presupposes a reason, a cause, a motive. If you're the one who killed him, the motive is there. And the reward… the very fact that tomorrow you would have had to pay a sum you didn't have…"

Aurigi boldly interrupted him.

"Who says I didn't have it?"

De Vincenzi immediately became insinuating while continuing to scrutinize him.

"So, did you pay?"

"You know whether I did or not!"

"No! Clearly I don't, or at least I don't know at this stage. What makes you think I might know?"

"Oh, well then…"

"Well then, you are the one who must tell me. And you must also demonstrate to me how you came by the money to pay, if you did."

The answer came immediately. Too quickly, and brimming with anxiety.

"I did not pay! How could I have come by the money to pay?"

De Vincenzi then remembered one of the two sheets of paper he'd found in the dead man's pocket and stuffed into his own as soon as he'd read them. He hadn't shown it even to Maccari.

And for the time being he hadn't shown it to the investigating magistrate, either. He instinctively went to draw the paper from his pocket. But all at once he held back. He didn't have to show it to Giannetto *yet*. He mustn't, if only because to do so would be procedurally irregular.

So he spoke again with renewed warmth, as if to excuse his own severity and the coldness he had to maintain during an investigation. This time, because of his friendship with Giannetto, it was troubling him.

"But good God, don't lock yourself up and lose yourself in some bitter and terrible silence! Don't you see that everyone is accusing you? How do you explain Garlini's coming here, if not with you or to find you here?"

"I don't know!"

"You're acting crazy. Are you hoping to get out of it by feigning insanity?"

Aurigi's eyes widened, as if the insinuation alone were powerful enough to stun him.

"But I'm not defending myself! I'm not defending myself. I'm only asking you not to torture me. If there's some of our old friendship left in you, if you can just manage not to despise me, don't keep on hoping to find out what I can't tell you, *because I don't know!*"

He fell back onto the sofa and took his head in his hands. A sob came from him and his words were pleading: "I cannot... I can't tell you anything! I don't know... I don't understand... I'm afraid to understand."

His head jerked upright in desperation. A quiet anguish could be heard in his voice. "I'm afraid—do you understand? *I'm frightened of knowing what happened in here!*"

De Vincenzi continued to stare at him. The entire drama could be summed up in those words. And Giannetto wouldn't utter any others, which were needed for explanation. Better to pretend not to want to know, and not acknowledge that things could now turn nasty.

"Fine. Calm down… after all, I'll manage on my own, even if you don't want me to. We have too many clues not to succeed."

He was looking for the right words. All at once, he deliberately put his hand in his pocket and took out not the piece of paper he'd fingered before without daring to show it to Aurigi, but another—the second of the two he'd found in the dead man's pocket. Now he held it before Giannetto's eyes.

"Look."

There was no need to tell him. Giannetto had seen it. He trembled long and hard.

He asked in a steady voice, "Was that in his pocket?"

"Yes. He had it in his pocket, the inside pocket of his tailcoat. It's yours, right? A note from you to Garlini, with yesterday's date on it. There's your signature. It says—"

Giannetto interrupted him sarcastically. He'd managed to overcome his shock and stated coldly, "I know what it says."

But De Vincenzi read it out: *"Come tonight at half-past midnight… Be ready to honour your commitment…* and the signature, your signature. So?"

The questions and answers, the words of these two men now chased each other round, retorting like shots from a revolver.

"It's obvious, no?" Giannetto uttered with all his sarcasm. "What more do you want?"

"It's absolutely clear… enough to send you to the firing squad."

"Oh!" And Giannetto hunched his shoulders, immediately adding coldly and decidedly, "He was a rogue. I killed him. Is that what everyone wants to believe? Now you know. Enough! It's over. I have nothing else to say to you."

"OK, but in fact it's not over. There's your alibi: you left La Scala at eleven-thirty and spent two hours walking around. People saw you."

The other man lit up with hope, almost despite himself. "Who saw me?"

His anxiety was so obvious that De Vincenzi felt once more as if he were on the wrong track. He had to ask: "But then… so you actually spent two hours wandering around Milan? Have you really told me the truth?"

"Ah!"

After all, the inspector knew nothing. No one had seen Aurigi wandering around Milan during that time. Giannetto fell back into his apathetic resignation.

"You see! No one saw me. And anyway, what would that prove? I could have killed him before starting out on my walk… right away… I wouldn't have stayed here staring at the body."

He would have gone on, but De Vincenzi interrupted him.

"Tell me, do you know Remigio Altieri? At least you can tell me that, no?"

Aurigi stopped and looked at him. He didn't understand.

"Remigio Altieri?" he asked, completely dumbfounded.

"Yes. A young blond man who lives—"

For some unknown reason, the inspector interrupted himself mid-flow, and held back from telling Aurigi where Remigio lived.

"No. I've never heard of him," Aurigi affirmed with sincerity.

Just then the doorbell rang. Giannetto quivered, instinctively stepping backwards as if moving out of harm's way.

Both men stood looking beyond the door of the room to the door of the apartment. It was opening.

From that moment on, the door took on the function of Destiny, determining the course of events each time it swung open like a terrible Nemesis.

7

Count Marchionni

The first to enter was a distinguished older man. He stood strong and erect, with an almost youthful elegance. Following him was a very small, slight man, who would nevertheless have turned heads in the street, his light grey suit was so flashy. His whole manner attracted attention. He wore rings on his fingers and a huge diamond on his brightly coloured cravat, and above that fantastic diamond and no less fantastic cravat was a common, ferret-like face, perpetually sniffing.

Cruni moved aside to let them in and closed the door behind them.

The elderly man came forward confidently. "I'd like to speak to the inspector in charge of the investigation. They told me at the station that he was here. I am Count Marchionni."

His face was serious and cryptic. When he saw Giannetto, he moved not a muscle.

De Vincenzi instantly recovered his calm assurance. He went towards the unexpected arrivals and bowed coldly.

"Inspector De Vincenzi. I'm at your service."

He then looked at Harrington and an ironic smile broke out on his face. "You've found something to do, Harrington!"

With a slight air of triumph the bejewelled man swiftly proclaimed: "I have the authorization of the chief constable, sir. The count has requested and obtained it!" He raised himself up on his heels.

"Precisely so," Count Marchionni confirmed. "I fancied I'd avail myself of Harrington's services. It's not that I don't have faith in the intelligence or ability of the functionaries working for Public Safety, but I think a private detective should be able to work freely. He can succeed where others fail. I've spent a lot of time living in England, and I am accustomed to considering the profession of private detective as necessary and indispensable."

He paused, as if waiting for the inspector to raise some objection. But De Vincenzi kept quiet, so he continued.

"The chief constable made an effort to understand my reasoning and he realized above all how crucial it is for me to know the truth, the whole truth. Only then will I be able to protect my daughter's honour from the slander and ugly comments being levelled against it."

Giannetto, who had remained silent and motionless in a corner of the room, took a step forward. His face became paler still, if that were possible, and his eyes gleamed.

But De Vincenzi quickly stepped between him and Marchionni, fearing that Aurigi might lose control of himself. He said quickly, "I don't understand, Count, how your daughter's honour can even vaguely be an issue."

"Until yesterday, my daughter was engaged to the killer."

At the word *killer*, even De Vincenzi was visibly shocked.

Aurigi's voice resounded with dull pain. "You can't believe I'm a killer!"

Marchionni slowly turned towards him. "I don't believe anything. I'm observing, trying to get to the bottom of this. I'm evaluating the situation. It's for others to condemn."

De Vincenzi intervened authoritatively. "Allow me, Count…" and he held up his hand, as if to prevent him physically from continuing.

He then turned towards the other side of the room and called Cruni. "Come here, sergeant."

Cruni came into the room. The inspector indicated Giannetto.

"Signor Aurigi is under arrest. I entrust him to you, Cruni. Take him there, into the dining room, to await transfer to San Fedele. He must not speak with anyone. Close the door and don't leave his side for any reason—not even for an instant."

Giannetto listened to the words with complete indifference. He fell back into his state of torpor and offered not the least resistance when the sergeant came towards him and said courteously, "Come with me."

They both disappeared into the dining room. Cruni closed the door.

All of this took place in seconds. The count witnessed it with no sign of surprise. The silence that followed was brief.

Casually, De Vincenzi offered Marchionni a chair. "Would you like to sit down, Count? Since you've gone against my wishes in coming here, I would like to ask you some questions."

"I'm here for that reason as well," the count replied as he sat.

De Vincenzi addressed Harrington.

"I believe you'll want to take a look at the crime scene, Harrington. Since you're authorized to follow the investigation, I'll allow it. But do understand that the investigating magistrate will do with you as he wishes. For the moment, you aren't bothering me in the least."

The detective immediately assumed a friendly, confidential air.

"I hope, instead, to be of some help, sir. I know a bit more than this morning's newspapers have published and I can tell you I already have a theory."

"A theory, eh, Harrington?" said De Vincenzi with a faintly ironic smile. "It's nice to have a theory... You should know that I, on the other hand, have no theory."

The other man ignored the inspector's irony. "Oh, you have only to get the little grey cells of your brain working!"

"That's it," said De Vincenzi. But then he broke off and said coldly, "So make them work, Harrington. Now is the moment to do so."

He started for the door of the parlour and signalled to the detective to follow him. At the threshold, he pointed inside and said, "The body was found here, in this room. Do go in but don't touch anything... in any case, we've already touched anything there was to touch."

Harrington entered the room and murmured, "I can believe it, sir."

De Vincenzi immediately turned to the count.

"Pardon me. As you see, I'm facilitating your detective's duties... a good man, that Harrington. He's been so anxious to start investigating a crime, a real crime. Give yourself an English name, like Sherlock Holmes, and you get involved only in information or surveillance... A martyr! But the good Lord has finally helped him out."

He paused. Then, looking closely at Marchionni, he asked, "But how do you think the work of a private detective can help you, Count?"

"He might be of some help to the police and therefore speed up the investigation."

There was sarcasm in his voice, but De Vincenzi seemed not to notice it and replied with perfect sincerity, "Thank you."

"And then he might show everyone, if the need arises, that even though Giannetto Aurigi is his daughter's fiancé, Count Marchionni has not hesitated to take a stand against him."

"Assuming he's actually guilty," the inspector insinuated with a gentle smile.

The count looked at him attentively, almost marvelling.

"Oh, yes, naturally. Well, sadly, what hope can there be of his innocence? Have you found something? When will there be an inquest?"

"We're at the beginning, as far as I'm concerned, at the beginning," De Vincenzi replied, shaking his head. "As for the investigating magistrate, I don't believe he's even begun yet, aside from the formalities."

"You see! No, no, I don't believe one can have any illusions about it…" Marchionni stopped talking and bowed his head.

"It's a complex crime, and terribly mysterious," the inspector observed, if only to break the embarrassing silence. "Everything seems to point to Aurigi. It's impossible to think who it could be if not him. And yet, logic balks at the idea."

"Indeed, anyone who'd known him up until yesterday, anyone who'd trusted him completely, to the extent of welcoming him into their own family, would refuse to believe he was guilty. But for that very reason I fear that this time, reason is being confused with sentiment… or with personal advantage, and I considered it my duty to make a useful and concrete contribution to unveiling the truth."

De Vincenzi's irony was now obvious. "By engaging our friend Harrington's investigative and deductive gifts?"

The count rose and said rather heatedly: "Precisely! In any case, he will act as a witness."

"For us"—De Vincenzi was frosty—"there wasn't any need for a witness."

"Given your reasoning, Inspector, which can be said to be driven neither by sentiment nor by gain, why do you hesitate to accept the evidence... which is there, all of it implicating Aurigi?"

"Because it would be the first time a criminal had brought his intelligence and strategy into play in order to render his own guilt absolutely clear."

"Well," said Marchionni, shrugging his shoulders, "even if he were a killer, Aurigi would only be an accidental one."

"Yes, but if one dismisses the idea of premeditation in this crime, it couldn't have happened. And if one allows for it, it couldn't have been carried out the way it appears to have been."

"By Jove!" exclaimed the count. The inspector's words seemed to have embarrassed him rather than anything else. To change the subject, and as if to get down to practicalities and confront the situation directly, he straightened up and said, "But you wanted to question me."

De Vincenzi corrected him with too much courtesy to be sincere. "I requested an interview with you. I wouldn't have allowed myself to question you. But I won't hide the fact that I'm relying on whatever you want to tell me to make progress with the investigation."

"I don't know how, but you may begin."

De Vincenzi seemed to be gathering himself together for a moment. Then, fixing his interviewee in the eye, he asked, "Yesterday evening, Giannetto Aurigi was with all of you at La Scala—in your box?"

"Aurigi is my daughter's fiancé. I could try to justify this fact, which I cannot deny. But I prefer not to. She has been engaged for a year. She would have got married after Lent. I assure you, however, that I had already decided that the marriage would not happen."

"Why? If you don't mind telling me…"

"For the past few months Aurigi has been gambling. Last month he made a huge loss on the stock market. This month the situation was even worse. Even if it hadn't happened… after what *had* happened he would never have been able to avoid ruin."

"I see," said De Vincenzi. "And what time did Aurigi leave the theatre last night?"

"After the second act of *Aida*. It must have been eleven."

"Was he in the foyer with you?"

"That is clear enough," Marchionni acknowledged with a brief smile. "It was I who invited him to come with me to the foyer for a conversation. The argument was heated, as heated as an argument in the foyer of La Scala can be, with all those people surrounding you, listening."

"And from the foyer, Aurigi went on to leave the theatre?"

"No. He returned to the box. He stayed with my wife and daughter for a few minutes and then he bid us goodbye and left, saying he had a sudden headache."

"You stayed in the box with the ladies?"

"Yes, naturally."

De Vincenzi noticed that for the first time since he'd started giving his answers, Marchionni had shown some slight embarrassment. He stared at him.

The count pressed ahead. "In the meantime, the third act had begun... my daughter went to visit the Marchesa di Belmonte in her box and remained with her friend, the Marchesa's daughter, until the end of the opera. She left the theatre with them and came back home in the Marchesa's automobile."

"I see," murmured the inspector. "Therefore, your daughter came back to your palazzo at around one in the morning."

"I make it exactly that time."

"Did you see her come in?" De Vincenzi asked immediately, watching him closely.

"Yes. But why are you asking these questions? I don't see how what I did with my family last night can interest you."

"Exactly! It doesn't. It's only to get the timing right and to try to understand Aurigi's movements that I'm asking how and where you and your family spent the evening."

"If you'd really like to know, then I'll tell you that after the show, I went to the Savini and then to the Clubino... I left the Clubino at two... or around two."

"Oh!" exclaimed De Vincenzi. "Strange."

The other man was sarcastic. "What's strange? That I surrendered to a premonition, and was away from home at just the time when a homicide was being committed?"

"I believe in premonitions," said De Vincenzi.

"But I don't. And I'll tell you that it was quite simply the argument I had with Aurigi that disturbed me. I felt he was hurtling towards his own ruin. I actually feared the worst, and

I was worried about the effect on my daughter of a definitive separation. It was already inevitable."

The count paced the room for several minutes before deliberately stopping in front of the inspector.

"My daughter loved her fiancé," he stated with some force. "She had chosen him freely. She would have renounced her title in order to marry him."

He went silent, waiting for De Vincenzi to say something. De Vincenzi kept quiet, so he began pacing the room once more, speaking to himself as if he'd forgotten that he was not alone.

"Certainly, I'd never have been able to think of something so terrible… but I knew that Aurigi was in the most serious financial difficulties… I saw him reduced to ruin… to bankruptcy… to flight, perhaps… I knew Maria Giovanna had had a violent confrontation with him just yesterday evening… I saw them speaking animatedly in the box and in the corridor."

He stopped once more and looked at De Vincenzi, who was still quiet, watching him.

"Premonition, eh?" he said with a bitter sneer. "Intuition. What's strange about my feeling nervous and upset?"

De Vincenzi thought he'd kept quiet for long enough.

"It wasn't for that premonition of yours that I exclaimed: 'Strange!'," he said in a calm voice. "The strangeness lies elsewhere."

The count was put on the defensive. "Explain yourself."

"I was saying that it's strange you could be there to see your daughter return home at one if you were at the Savini or the Clubino."

The count was not terribly perturbed. He smiled. "Oh, so that's it? In fact, I did not see her come back. The porter

91

told me what time she came back last night and my wife confirmed it. Does any of this seem to you to be of the slightest significance?"

"None," De Vincenzi said offhandedly.

"Exactly! None. And I don't see why you should trouble your brain excessively in order to reconstruct the scene of the crime."

"So you think. Yes, there can be more than one logical reconstruction. But all of them ring false, like cracked bells."

Marchionni gave him a look of sincere commiseration. "So you've come to this conclusion!"

"No. I've not yet come to any conclusion... I'm still working on it."

"Very well," the count said coolly, as if to cut their conversation short. "But you'll let Harrington look, and you won't hinder his progress, isn't that right?"

"Certainly not. Because *he is really seeking proof of the truth.*"

The count started for the parlour door. "I'm going to tell him, then, if you'll allow it."

De Vincenzi bowed. "But of course."

When he got to the door, he called him back.

"Excuse me, Count. Might I possibly telephone the Contessa to ask her to receive me?"

Marchionni slowly turned. He looked at De Vincenzi with perfect composure.

"You cannot telephone the palazzo, Inspector." He paused calculatedly.

Marchionni certainly is a clever man, De Vincenzi thought to himself. He understood perfectly what De Vincenzi was getting at with his request. And in fact he continued, with a hint of irony. "We don't have a telephone. I've never wanted to install one."

"Then, if you don't mind, would you notify her of my visit yourself?"

"Naturally. I'll tell my wife about it and you can come today, this afternoon."

He answered De Vincenzi's bow with a nod of his head, and disappeared into the parlour.

De Vincenzi stood still, lost in thought. The interview had opened up a new horizon. New, and rather unsettling. Where would things end up? At the moment, the drama was running down tortuous paths strewn with obstacles of every kind. Evidently, that gentleman had a plan, and it surely wasn't the one he'd admitted to. De Vincenzi remembered the comparison he'd already made, and thought that Marchionni, too, rang as false as a cracked bell.

But why? Where was the crack in him, and what had caused it?

He paused before walking to the door of the dining room. He looked inside and signalled for Cruni to join him. He then closed the door straightaway. When the sergeant was beside him, he took his arm confidentially and said quietly, "Cruni, my friend... you trust me, right?"

He always used a little of the familiar *tu* with him as well as the more formal *voi*, according to whim.

Neither the words nor the tone of his superior surprised Cruni. He understood him and was fond of him. As an inspector, De Vincenzi didn't harass his personal staff with too many demands. He was the only one who was always courteous with them. The only one who didn't let them take the blame for his own errors, or land them with all the tedium of the job.

"I've been with you for eight years, sir," he said, his voice betraying his emotion. "It's you who should trust me… I'd do anything to show myself worthy of it."

And he underlined the phrase vigorously, waving his fist around in the air.

A smile crossed De Vincenzi's face. "I know, Cruni. However, right now I'm actually relying on you. I have to…"

He hesitated briefly, staring into the eyes of his employee. He read in them such frankness that he immediately took up the thread again.

"Cruni, I'm about to do something irregular… quite irregular… and you must do it with me, if you don't mind. It's necessary. Not only to save that man in there—" and he indicated the dining room door "—if he actually deserves to be saved."

The sergeant interrupted. "Sir, that man hasn't killed anyone! I'll tell you that myself, and I mean it. He didn't kill anyone!"

De Vincenzi muttered, "I don't know, Cruni. I myself do not know. What I do know for sure, however, is that there is some aspect of this crime… actually its most horrible aspect… that has nothing to do with Aurigi. However, it's necessary, Cruni—do you understand?—it's necessary for me to see clearly right the way through. The usual means, legal, all the rules, are not enough, and they're not helpful in this case. I must have recourse to other methods if I want to get to the truth—to all other means, whatever they might be. My conscience will allow it, and in fact it obliges me, even if the rules and codes forbid it. So I need you. Are you willing to help me?"

"You can count on me!" said Cruni, putting a hand to his breast.

"Yes, I'm counting on you. Now I'll tell you what has to be done, but first get me an officer. There should be two at the main door. Get the sharpest ones."

The sergeant quickly went out of the back door, leaving the entrance door open.

De Vincenzi glanced at the door to the dining room. He slowly approached it, listening. He could hear a pin drop. He opened it a crack and saw Giannetto sitting in front of the table, his head between his hands. He wasn't moving and he didn't move even when the door opened.

De Vincenzi smiled bitterly. He closed the door and returned to the middle of the room. He looked at Aurigi once more, and this time he was angry. Why did he persist in keeping his silence? Why was it up to him to save Aurigi at all costs?

Cruni came into the apartment with an officer. De Vincenzi looked at the latter and said, "Right. You, go and stand in that room," and he pointed towards the dining room. "You'll find a gentleman under arrest in there. You are answerable to me for him. But take care to treat him courteously and, above all, try to give him the impression that you're not there and you aren't watching him. Lock the door from the inside if you need to, and don't let anyone in other than the investigating magistrate, of course. But I'll see him first myself. Understood?"

The officer bowed, throwing his arms out in an awkwardly expressive gesture, "Yes, sir!"

"Go." And De Vincenzi went with him, closing the door behind him.

Then he went up to Cruni. "Now, listen."

Quickly and with the greatest possible clarity, De Vincenzi laid out the essential points of Marchionni's statement and asked Cruni to verify them. He would go to the Savini, the Clubino, to the count's palazzo and interrogate all who might confirm or deny what Marchionni had said. He advised him, though, to use the utmost discretion. Cruni had to realize that he, as well as the inspector, was playing a dangerous game by verifying the statement of such an important witness in that way.

Cruni responded by nodding his assent. He understood perfectly. At one point he exclaimed, "That gentleman doesn't seem very Christian to me either."

"Christian or not, dear Cruni, if the chief constable hears what we're doing without his authorization, he'll blow up at us. For me it's nothing, but for you…"

"Oh, for me," the sergeant shrugged his shoulders. And taking up his hat, which he'd set on a chair at the entrance, he headed for the door.

At precisely that moment, a key was inserted into the lock from the outside. The noise it made as it turned was sharp and clear.

De Vincenzi suddenly grabbed Cruni's arm and drew him into a corner. They stood flat against the wall, their eyes fixed on the door.

The key turned twice, and the door slowly opened.

8

The Two Revolvers

One side of the double doors opened to frame the shape of a square, thickset man. His grey hair was practically in his eyes and he was wearing a long overcoat.

He stopped for an instant to look round the entrance hall, but he didn't see the two men hiding behind the door to the kitchen. He advanced slowly, carefully closing the door behind him. Then he proceeded towards the servant's room and took off his overcoat and hat. From the bed he took a blue-and-white-striped vest and a black jacket. He looked at his garments for a moment as if considering whether or not he had to put them on, and then decided. He took off the clothes he was wearing and got dressed in the others, which clearly indicated his function.

He then went towards the dining room.

De Vincenzi could see him clearly. A rather elderly man with grey hair, but good skin, still plump and fresh.

The inspector didn't let him go into the dining room. When he got to the middle of the entrance hall, he went straight up to him.

The man jumped and instinctively put his hand to the rear pocket of his trousers. In a voice that was threatening, though not terribly perturbed, he asked: "What are you doing in here?"

The inspector asked, "Are you Giacomo Macchi, Aurigi's servant?"

The man was startled but immediately regained his self-confidence.

"I am, in fact, Signor Aurigi's servant. But who are you, and what are you doing in my master's house?"

"I will tell you later," answered De Vincenzi, heading towards the dining room. "Come along, now, give me the revolver you have in your pocket and answer my questions."

"Who gave you the right?"

"I am a police inspector. Quickly, the revolver."

The servant vacillated. He struggled to gain control of himself, take the revolver from his pocket and offer it to De Vincenzi.

"I don't understand…"

"You will," said De Vincenzi. He inspected the revolver. "A Browning… 6.5… with seven bullets." He twisted the barrel to make sure the bullets were there and sniffed the muzzle. The revolver had definitely not been shot recently.

"A nice weapon, perfectly maintained. Give me the gun licence."

"I don't have it," the servant responded after a moment's hesitation.

"Fine. And the revolver is yours?"

"Yes… no… it's not mine."

"Whose is it then?"

"It's Signor Aurigi's… my master's."

"So why are you carrying it?"

"I took it yesterday evening. I'd hoped to put it back in its place this morning. He wouldn't have noticed."

"Where does he normally keep it?"

The servant turned and pointed to a small chest of drawers in the corner, close to the mantelpiece, where the clock was sounding a quarter to ten.

"There, in the top drawer of that chest."

De Vincenzi went over to the chest and tried to open the drawer. It was locked. He turned to Giacomo.

"The key?"

The servant was clearly surprised. "I don't know! It was open… it's always open…"

He went up to the chest and opened some of the other drawers to look for the key.

"I don't understand! Last night it was open and the key was in the lock."

De Vincenzi turned to Cruni. "Get a chisel, some sort of tool. There must be a chisel in the house, a hammer, something to open this drawer."

"Yes," said Macchi, "there's a toolbox in the kitchen, in the cupboard. I'll go and get it."

De Vincenzi held him by the arm. "No. Stay here." And he signalled for Cruni to go to the kitchen.

The inspector, still holding Giacomo by the arm, looked him in the eye: "You say it was open last night?"

"Of course. Signor Aurigi always leaves all his drawers open. He knows he can trust me."

"Indeed," the inspector said ironically.

The other man raised his shoulders. "I told you I would have put it back. If I'd asked to borrow it, he would have given it to me."

"Why did you need a revolver last night?"

Giacomo was silent.

"Why?" the inspector insisted.

"Oh," the servant said with some effort, "I don't know why you're asking me all these questions. You found the revolver on me. I don't have a licence for it. So arrest me if you wish. I have nothing else to say."

"Ah, you think so?"

Cruni came in with a chisel. The inspector took it from him brusquely.

"Give it here…"

He bent over the drawer and opened it by jiggling the latch. He looked inside and expressed amazement. He turned to Giacomo.

"Oh, I say! If you are toying with me, my good man, you'll regret it."

The servant looked at him in surprise.

"Me? But what are you saying?"

"Watch it!" said De Vincenzi. He took another revolver from the drawer. "And this one here, whose is it? Did your master have a collection of revolvers?"

Giacomo seemed totally amazed.

"But no! Only one. That one wasn't there! No, I've never seen that one, sir. Let me have a look…" He held out his hand.

De Vincenzi was about to give it to him but he stopped himself.

He studied the revolver, sniffed the end as he'd done with the other, and nodded.

"Wait!"

The revolver he'd taken from Giacomo was sitting on the table. He wrapped it in his handkerchief for the second time and put it in his pocket.

He turned to Cruni.

"Telephone the doctor at the Monumentale cemetery right away, and ask him to send me the bullet he's removed. And then find me a gunsmith who'll—"

He looked at the clock on the mantelpiece, smiled, and took his own watch from his pocket. Yes, the clock was actually an hour ahead.

He went on, turning back to Cruni "—who'll come here at eleven. As soon as you've done that, go you-know-where and do what I told you."

"Right, sir," said Cruni, starting for the entrance. "Do you want me to have Paoli come up here to see you?"

"It's not important. Just tell him not to move from the lodge for any reason."

The inspector waited for the sergeant to leave and then turned to Giacomo.

"And now, it's just us." He sat down and showed the servant a seat.

"Please sit down. There are a lot of things I need you to tell me. What time did you go out last night?"

Giacomo remained standing.

"At eleven. My master had given me permission. He knew I wouldn't come back before this morning."

De Vincenzi was startled. "Oh, he knew that?"

"Of course," said Macchi. "Yesterday morning he himself said I'd have free time. Every week Signor Aurigi gives me a night off. Usually it's Friday night. This week he wanted to change it. Yesterday morning, he said, 'Giacomo, today is Tuesday, but it doesn't matter. You're free tonight instead of Friday. I prefer it that way.'"

Silence fell. De Vincenzi said to himself that the further the investigation advanced, the more it seemed to demonstrate Aurigi's guilt.

"And you take the revolver away with you every week?"

"Yes. What's wrong with that? I go to a house in the Cagnola zone, five minutes' walk from the station at the end of the line—at night."

"And Aurigi has never noticed that you've taken his revolver away—as a precaution?"

"No, never! I told you: he's never had occasion to use the revolver."

"Fine. We'll check up on what you say. But be careful. A crime was committed in this house last night…"

The servant took a step backwards. The terror written all over his face had to be sincere, thought De Vincenzi, or else the man was a hardened criminal, a consummate actor.

"No!" he exclaimed in a hoarse voice. "My master?"

"Not your master. He is safe and sound. But be aware that everything you tell us, including your alibi, is extremely important."

"It goes without saying." He didn't even try to hide his distress. His fear must have preyed on him.

"I'm saying exactly what I mean," De Vincenzi stated coldly. "But your only concern is to tell the truth."

The man looked around him, lost. "But who? Who? And where is my master?"

"Sit down," ordered the inspector, and this time the man sat down automatically.

"Were you at home all day yesterday?"

"Yes."

"Tell me what happened in here yesterday afternoon."

"But... I don't know," Giacomo answered, shrugging. "Nothing unusual, I believe."

"Aurigi went out at three?"

"Yes, at three... or maybe later... No, I think it was actually at three."

"And while he was out, someone came."

"You know?" Giacomo exclaimed in surprise. Immediately he added, "Yes, *la signorina* came. I'd told her that my master was out and let her come in here, in this room. Nothing strange there, as far as it goes. When Signor Aurigi isn't at home, the signorina always comes in here... or there, in the parlour, and waits for him."

"Does she come every day, the signorina?"

"But no!" Giacomo said, amazed. "Why would she come every day?"

De Vincenzi studied him. Which of the two was lying—this man, or the porter's wife? She had said that the signorina came every day.

"Take care. Try to be absolutely precise. It seems to me she comes every day."

The servant shrugged. "If that's what you think."

The inspector realized he was dealing with a particularly nervous and touchy customer. He would need to get on the right side of him.

"Good. We're going to find out the truth. If not every day, when?"

"Oh, rarely. Once a week, for example, or less often or more frequently, depending. And then, her visits are always really brief. She stays with the signore in this room or there in the dining room. They talk, but the signorina is always in a great hurry. The signore was never happy about that, naturally."

It was clear that the man wasn't lying, at least on this point. Why would he lie anyway?

But in that case, how could one square the porter's wife's statement with the servant's?

The porter's wife couldn't be lying, either. She had been too frightened to do so at the time. And anyway, even if she'd wanted to for reasons of her own, she *would have lied* by denying the fact as she'd tried to do in the beginning, not admitting it. She was clearly receiving money from Aurigi or from the Signorina Marchionni, and one never confesses to such a thing voluntarily.

What then?

De Vincenzi had to allow that *the contessina might have come through Aurigi's door without visiting her fiancé.*

It was an arbitrary theory. But wasn't everything about real life and reality a bit arbitrary?

It was a problem, this, which the inspector set aside to study and resolve later. For the moment, the important thing was to get the man in front of him to speak.

"And so? Go on."

"After half an hour... or perhaps more... I heard the bell again. It was my master with a gentleman—"

He stopped himself. A look flashed across his face. He got up, deeply unsettled.

"But no! It isn't possible..."

De Vincenzi got up too and looked Giacomo in the eye.

"What's not possible?" He held up a hand to stop Macchi. "No, don't answer, I'm not interested in what you think is possible or impossible. Give me the facts. Who was that gentleman?"

The servant had recovered some of his sang-froid.

"The signorina's father. Count Marchionni. When I saw him, I immediately said to myself that I had to warn my master. He might not have wanted the father to encounter his own daughter here, I thought. And I tried signalling to him not to enter this room, but he didn't understand me."

"So they came in. And did they find the signorina?"

"No, no… the signorina must have heard their voices… I don't know… the fact is that she hid in there, in the dining room."

De Vincenzi leapt up. It seemed he was beginning to understand.

"Ah! And then?"

"My master and the count remained in this room for a long time. A few hours. They were arguing."

De Vincenzi held up a hand to interrupt him once more. He stared at the door of the parlour. He went up to it and looked inside, but saw neither Marchionni nor Harrington. They must have been in the bedroom or the bathroom. He seemed satisfied and carefully shut the door of the parlour. Then he turned to the servant and said in a hushed tone, "So they were arguing. Loudly?"

"Yes… like that… every now and again you could hear a voice break out, grow hushed, then start up again speaking calmly."

"And the signorina?"

"She stayed in there for half an hour. Then all of a sudden I saw her go out through the door that leads into the kitchen. She was white as a sheet. She said to me: 'Giacomo, you'll say to your master that I came and couldn't wait. I'll see him tonight at the theatre.' I saw her to the door on the stairs, making sure this door was closed and that the men in the dining room couldn't see her. That's how the signorina left. And that's all."

"Her father didn't see her?"

"No, I don't believe so."

"And when your master and the count were speaking, you naturally…"

From the parlour came the voices of Harrington and the count.

De Vincenzi rapidly went up to Macchi and pushed him towards the entrance.

"Enough! We'll continue later."

The door of the parlour opened and the count appeared with Harrington. Marchionni made straight for De Vincenzi. He still had a somewhat sarcastic air and he asked De Vincenzi with a hiss: "That room was searched thoroughly, is that right, Inspector?"

Then he noticed Giacomo. He pointed to him. "This man is the servant of… for…"

"Yes, Count," De Vincenzi interrupted. "This man is Aurigi's servant, and naturally you must know him, since you had occasion to see him yesterday afternoon."

The count was visibly startled, but he quickly got the better of his agitation.

"That may be, but I don't think it's anything important. What seems terribly important, however, is what Harrington has to say to you."

"Ah. Has Harrington managed to perfect his theory?"

Ever more vacuous and triumphant, the detective answered, "Just a few points, sir—and to reach this outcome I did nothing but observe. They moved everything, but as one knows, something can escape notice! For example, on the floor in the parlour, under an armchair, I found this…"

De Vincenzi took the stub and examined it. Then, lifting his head, he let out a little whistle. He looked at Harrington. Poor thing, he thought to himself, at least we can let him have this satisfaction.

Aloud he said, "The other half of a ticket for a seat at La Scala."

"Number 34H. On the right. Yesterday's date," the detective remarked triumphantly. A keen joy was depicted on his tiny, gnarled face, which shone so brightly as to eclipse the beams from the huge diamond on his cravat for just a moment.

The count intervened in a frosty voice. "Aurigi's seat."

De Vincenzi turned towards Marchionni with a smile. "I know very well that you are not mistaken in saying that it was Aurigi's seat."

"Of course I'm not mistaken! During the first act, before coming to our box, Aurigi was in that seat and I remember very well which row it was."

"Of course, but of course," said De Vincenzi. "So we can say this is proof… proof that Aurigi came in here after having been to the theatre."

"Here, in his own house, and in that parlour," Harrington emphasized.

"Right," De Vincenzi murmured, pensive.

After a short silence, he turned to the detective. "So, Harrington, explain your theory to me."

"Oh! I don't believe I'm revealing any great thing when I say that—"

He'd adopted the pose of an orator, and was about to get his own back when the telephone rang in the entrance hall.

"Allow me," De Vincenzi said, and quickly made for the other side of the room.

He picked up the receiver and a short time later could be heard to speak.

"Hello… Yes… It's me, *commendatore*… Oh, for now, nothing… I'll be with you by midday and I'll report to you then… No, not so easily… of course! I won't make statements of any kind to the press. Oh, they've already brought you the results of the examination?… Yes, thank you… What did you say?… In the purchase ledger? Under yesterday's date… Curious… I mean that it's curious and incredible. I'll explain later, *commendatore*. Goodbye."

He put down the receiver and stood for a moment looking into space. So? Certainly what the chief of police had told him was deeply troubling. He had to stay in the hallway for a moment since he did not want to reveal the level of his disturbance to the other two.

Finally, he returned to the dining room.

"So, we were saying," he spoke hurriedly. "Actually it was you, Harrington, who were ready to explain your theory. And?"

Harrington resumed his pose.

"I was saying that the clues and the evidence… deduction and common sense… the entire picture of the crime… the timings… the motives… the psychology of the people involved… everything serves to demonstrate that the killer is one person and could only be Aurigi."

De Vincenzi sat down, looking at and listening to Harrington with ostentatious interest.

"Yes," he said, interrupting him. "Therefore, Aurigi would have made an appointment with Garlini in his own house…

he'd have come here from the theatre... and he'd have met the banker here... and he'd have killed him... Is that it?"

Harrington didn't notice the sarcasm in the inspector's words, and he emphatically exclaimed: "By Jove!"

"And in your view, the motive for the crime—what would that be?" the inspector asked calmly.

The other man lifted his shoulders sympathetically. "The money! In a couple of days, Aurigi would have had to pay Garlini—note this—several hundred thousand lire, which he didn't have."

"Do you think so?" De Vincenzi asked sarcastically.

"But I know this myself," the count interrupted. "I don't think so, I know it!"

De Vincenzi got up and said with perfect courtesy, "Allow me to tell you, Count, that you are mistaken, as we all were. The person on the phone two minutes ago was the chief of police. And he informed me that the most important discovery made by the experts was in the ledgers of the Garlini Bank."

He looked the two men in the face, pausing meaningfully.

"Aurigi," he continued, enunciating with care, "owed Garlini exactly five hundred and forty-three thousand lire."

"You see!" the count yelled triumphantly.

"I see," the inspector replied patiently. "But in Garlini's books it appears that, as of yesterday, that money was deposited."

"No!" and "That's impossible!" the count and Harrington exclaimed simultaneously. Their shock was so great that it had to be sincere.

Slowly, De Vincenzi drew the folded piece of paper from his pocket. He opened it and began to pore over it.

The other two watched him, profoundly amazed.

After a long pause, De Vincenzi said, "It's just possible, Count, that when I searched the clothes Garlini was wearing, I found this receipt. I'll read it to you: *I accept the sum of five hundred and forty-three thousand lire from Signor Giannetto Aurigi as the full amount to settle the negative balance in his share dealing carried over to the end of this December.*" He held out the receipt to the count. "See? Stamps and signature. Everything in order."

Now the count was shocked.

"And you say," he stuttered, "that this receipt…"

"Precisely. This receipt was found in the pocket of Garlini's evening jacket." He paused for a moment and then added, pointing to the right breast pocket: "In this breast pocket…"

"In that pocket? No, it wasn't there!" the count exclaimed with an involuntary shudder.

De Vincenzi immediately replied, "In fact, not in that pocket. It was in another… But Count Marchionni, how did you know it wasn't there?"

The count was furious.

Shocked, Harrington took a step backwards, in an effort to separate himself from his client.

An anxious silence hung over the room.

9

I Killed Him!

Not one of the four men in the room moved. De Vincenzi stood calm and serene, his hands in his pockets, watching the count unobtrusively.

He wished he could disregard the importance of the count's outburst. He wanted to strip the incident down, lay everything in a straight line. He didn't want to give undue weight to Marchionni's unconscious outburst, even though it revealed a deeply vulnerable, injured side to one of the drama's chief protagonists.

Marchionni calmed down instantly, almost as if he'd understood the inspector's thoughts. He kept still, displaying not the slightest emotion, not even breathing more rapidly. He appeared to be waiting, like De Vincenzi, for the facts to explain themselves.

Harrington was the most affected of all. His dazzling diamond had stolen the light from his eyes, which had gone dull, and all of the cunning had seeped from his now colourless face. He moved away from Marchionni, as though he wanted to distance himself from the affair. It was as if he accepted that the whole thing was getting the better of him, was much bigger than he was, and he had lost all desire to investigate it.

The last to arrive was the servant, Giacomo Macchi. He'd been on the sidelines until then, somehow removed by dint of his function. He stared at the ground, clearly more embarrassed than surprised or shocked by events that had begun with a death and now posed real danger, like a stick of dynamite.

De Vincenzi silently ran through the facts, trying to get his bearings with the urgency of a captain who fears a storm. There wasn't time for him to take out the sextant and make precise calculations. He had to go chiefly by intuition. It was through intuition—and almost unconsciously—that he'd drawn Marchionni into the trap, and when he had deliberately lied, stating that the receipt was found on the body in the breast pocket, not even De Vincenzi himself knew the value of that lie. It had unexpectedly borne fruit, but was it worth anything? Was it possible that the count had killed Garlini? Yes, it was possible. But one would need to find all the other missing elements of the case.

De Vincenzi was thinking, and he wanted simultaneously to ban himself from thinking. He really wished he could proceed unconsciously, like a dowser. He was looking for a killer, and he had to find him with a magic wand.

The silence continued to hang over those four stationary men. It was no longer an anxious silence, but almost cataleptic. Stagnant.

Was it possible to break through that turbid atmosphere? To leave and breathe fresh air again? How could one move in it?

Of course, it was chance that intervened as always, like a stone tossed into a pond.

The doorbell rang again—nervously—and they all jumped. Everyone unconsciously breathed a sigh of relief.

But the relief was short-lived.

All four were gripped by a further wave of anxiety. What sort of surprise, what new shock would come through the door when it was opened by the duty officer in the entrance hall?

The person who came in was a woman. She walked straight past the officer and into the dining room, not at all surprised to find all those men there, staring at her in amazement.

She was very beautiful and terribly young. Truly elegant, she held a golden purse in her gloved hands as she pulled her fur coat over her breast.

De Vincenzi looked at her, eyes wide, hardly able to breathe.

The woman in the photograph! The young blond man's girlfriend!

And yet she was also—he had no doubt—Giannetto Aurigi's fiancée.

The plot was leaping ahead, flashing like lightning.

This was the engagement ring. The top floor of the house— the neat and tidy attic—was about to be married to the second floor—Aurigi's bachelor apartment—where a body had been found.

The new link popped into De Vincenzi's head unexpectedly, and suggested a disturbing web of mysterious and hidden facts.

He was deeply shocked, and troubled by a nagging worry. That man under observation in the adjoining room, the man he'd had to declare under arrest—was he, therefore, not only innocent, but victim of an even greater misfortune, of which he was as yet unaware? One that was about to deliver a terrible, deep new blow? Or did he know about it, and did the entire plot hinge on his knowing it?

It wasn't possible! *Giannetto didn't even know Remigio Altieri by name.*

To think that a drama involving only three people—the fatal triangle, the magic circle of lovers' betrayal—might have repercussions on a fourth, who appeared to have no connection whatsoever apart from with one of them, and then only a financial one!

De Vincenzi had to struggle furiously to avoid showing his confusion.

Marchionni was the first to speak. At his daughter's entrance, the older man had jumped up and his face had gone livid.

"Why have you come here, Maria Giovanna?" he asked. His voice was hoarse and trembled with suppressed anxiety rather than anger.

The daughter looked straight at her father, somewhat astonished by the question.

"Why does it surprise you, Papa? I'm Giannetto Aurigi's fiancée."

The count's eyes shot sparks. "You are no longer his fiancée and you do not belong here. Go back home!"

"You are mistaken, Papa." And her voice remained clear and harmonious enough to convince one that she had forgotten what she knew. "Even if Giannetto had killed someone, I would not abandon him. But he hasn't killed anyone, and I know it."

"Keep quiet! You're mad, Maria Giovanna!"

This time his voice was brimming with rage. It was obvious that Marchionni could barely restrain himself from running up to his daughter and shutting her mouth with his own hand.

He turned to De Vincenzi with anguish in his voice, almost imploring, "Don't you listen to her! Don't listen to her! She doesn't know what she's saying!"

114

De Vincenzi watched him.

Slowly, and with the same simplicity, Maria Giovanna affirmed: "No. It wasn't Aurigi who killed Garlini. It was me!"

With those words, the drama was contained between the two: father and daughter. De Vincenzi had disappeared, along with the others who didn't figure in the drama. No one existed apart from the elderly gentleman, trembling with anger and horror, and his beautiful young girl. She was only slightly pale, but her lips were too bright, like an open wound in that pallor.

"Crazy! Crazy! Why are you lying? To save him?"

He wrung his hands convulsively. Still facing De Vincenzi, he begged, "Don't believe her! None of this makes any sense! My daughter wasn't here last night! She's lying to save him."

The young girl stepped forward determinedly.

She stated a truth she knew to be incontestable. "I was here! So why are you lying, Papa? In order to condemn him?"

The others were shocked.

Now the knife had really entered the wound, turned in it, and lacerated it.

The count had collapsed onto the sofa as if someone had clubbed him. He breathed with difficulty, his face in his hands.

Everyone was silent.

At that instant, the pendulum clock on the mantelpiece took the floor, slowly striking the hours, one after another.

De Vincenzi was startled by the sound. He stared at the clock and his eyes lit up as if in revelation. His lips moved silently, counting the hours.

As though he'd suggested it, the others followed the sound and did the same. Even the count had raised his head.

The clock struck eleven, then went quiet.

To conclude matters, De Vincenzi took out his own watch and looked at it as if he were doing a sum or putting a full stop after a sentence.

"It's ten," he said.

At that point the count, too, stood up. The others were surprised. Giacomo stepped back towards the door, but then stopped and went back to his previous position. The only person not to notice what was happening was Harrington.

The inspector seemed to have been relieved of a weight that had hampered his actions up to that point. He moved with newfound ease; everything he did was now simple, spontaneous and natural.

"Ladies and gentlemen," he said placidly, "I believe each of you, for different reasons, needs a bit of rest. One can't ask of one's nerves more than they can bear, or one risks stretching them to snapping point."

He turned his gaze on each face in turn and continued.

"The atmosphere in this room has reached white heat—a bad temperature for keeping one's brain working and a clear head. I myself fear that the very rhythm of your pulses is influencing my judgement. You'll understand, therefore, if I ask you to leave me alone with my thoughts. I must organize them and master them. All right?"

No one spoke. As if fearing that someone might break the silence, the inspector quickly added, "Thank you. I see you understand me. So…"

He looked around and addressed the count first.

"Count Marchionni, I wonder, would you go to this room."

And he pushed him towards the door of the parlour.

Marchionni had recovered his cool—along with his haughtiness. "What conclusion are you expecting to reach? I hope, considering how hot it's become, that your brain has helped to keep you from placing too much weight on my daughter's words of madness!"

"Of course," answered De Vincenzi, still gently pushing him towards the parlour. "You can be sure of that. I am, of course, *not meant to heed anyone's words*... Now more than ever, I feel that in any relationship with our fellow human beings, when indisputable proof is lacking... and indisputable proof does not exist, or hardly exists... *only when alone can one evaluate an individual's worth*. Do make yourself comfortable and wait in there."

When he reached the door, the count turned round.

"Does that mean you are detaining me?"

"Oh no. It means I'm asking you to stay here for a little while yet."

"Don't you worry about the consequences of liberty?"

"Liberty?" said De Vincenzi, truly amazed. "The meaning of the word is elastic."

"You believe so?"

And the sarcasm in that question stung like a lash. But De Vincenzi wasn't having it.

Marchionni shrugged. "Go ahead, in any case." And he disappeared into the parlour.

The inspector closed the door and turned to face the others. Harrington was nearest to him, and De Vincenzi pointed to the entrance:

"Harrington, I don't believe you have anything more to do here. See you later."

Harrington overcame his embarrassment enough to say,

"I don't intend to occupy myself further with this matter, Inspector. Someone else can let the chief constable know that it was made impossible for me to act—"

De Vincenzi interrupted him almost violently.

"No, Harrington! I'll take care of the matter myself now, but you'll get involved if I want you to be. In any case, I'd ask you to come to my office at three this afternoon. Goodbye."

And he accompanied Harrington to the door himself. He waited for him to leave and to start going downstairs before turning to the officer still waiting in the entrance hall.

"Follow him. There's no reason for it, but I want to teach him a lesson…"

The officer went off to follow the detective and De Vincenzi closed the door.

On his way back to the dining room he saw Giacomo heading for his own room, and he blocked his way.

"And where are you going?"

"I thought you didn't need me either."

"As it happens, I don't, but the house needs you and before long I will too. Go in there and don't do anything besides your work. Behave as if nothing has happened."

The servant shook his head. "I don't think it will be easy."

His voice frosty once more, the inspector ordered Macchi: "Well in any case it will be easy for you not to come in here until I call you."

Back in the drawing room, he closed the door carefully. His movements had slowed, as if he wanted to give his mind time to calm down completely. When he turned to Maria Giovanna, he was proper and polite. He smiled.

The young woman was the first to speak, and she wasn't the

least bit disturbed or intimidated by a man who presented himself as a proper interrogator.

"Where is Aurigi?"

"Not far away. Do you wish to speak to him?"

"I would be grateful to do so," whispered Maria Giovanna. She suddenly sounded insecure.

"To him first, or to me?" De Vincenzi asked, studying her.

"To you. You must have heard what I said..."

"Of course I heard it, but hearing doesn't mean understanding, and above all it does not mean believing."

The young woman begged him. "You must believe me! I'm telling the truth."

"A sad truth, signorina! Which, if it were actually so, would not save anything or anyone."

"Unfortunately by this point there's nothing left to save!"

Such was the desperation in her words that even De Vincenzi felt troubled by them.

"However," he said energetically, controlling himself, "I need to understand." He went on, his voice full of affection and cordiality, "And as for complete ruin, it's never as certain as it might seem when one is momentarily bewildered."

A long shudder coursed through the young woman. She kept quiet, trying to contain a surge of desperation that threatened to spill out of her. But she couldn't, and she covered her face with her hands.

"What's happened to me in a single day is terrible. You must have pity on me!"

"How could I fail to, signorina?"

He led her to an armchair and helped her to sit down. She moved like a robot. When he saw her nearly settled, he asked gently, "Why did you accuse yourself of killing Garlini, Signorina Marchionni?"

The young woman found a last surge of resistance.

"Because I did kill him!" she shouted.

"But *why* did you kill him—*you*?"

"Isn't it enough for me to tell you that I did it?"

But the inspector was looking at her so intently that she whispered without realizing, "There are things one doesn't confess to…"

"Yes… and sometimes it's easier to confess to a crime one has not committed."

Maria Giovanna watched him, then tossed her head and turned her gaze away. She seemed calm. With her hands on her knees, she looked up and said slowly, "You are wrong not to believe me. I really did kill Garlini."

De Vincenzi took a chair and sat down in front of her.

"Shall we say that you would benefit from extenuating circumstances if you had killed him?"

Maria Giovanna started. She looked the inspector straight in the face now, terrified, and she shouted at him, as if trying to distance herself from a threat.

"Why do you say that? What do you know? I beg you—tell me what you know!"

"Calm down. What I may know changes neither what happened nor the course of events."

Two tears appeared in Maria Giovanna's eyes.

"Oh, believe me, believe me, and don't try to find out anything else!"

"You physically killed a man by shooting him in the temple with a revolver…"

He uttered these words slowly, enunciating clearly, marking every syllable. He paused before suddenly getting up and walking towards the fireplace. He held out his hand to indicate the pendulum clock.

"And after you did all this, you, Contessina Marchionni, adjusted this clock, *so that it would show an hour ahead*?"

Profoundly amazed, Maria Giovanna asked, "What clock? What are you saying? I didn't touch that clock."

The inspector's yelp was triumphant.

"You see! You did not touch that clock. I was absolutely convinced of it. *And for that reason, you cannot have killed Garlini!*"

"But what are you saying? What does the clock have to do with anything?" Maria Giovanna repeated.

De Vincenzi recovered his calm indifference.

"Don't try to understand. And believe me, it's too difficult to get yourself convicted for a crime you did not commit. More difficult than getting convicted for one you *have* committed!" His tone was unchanged when he suddenly asked, "Contessina Marchionni, where were you last night from eleven-thirty until one?"

The cry of victory was now hers. "In this house!"

"I know," De Vincenzi said with the same tranquillity, and from his waistcoat pocket he took the little lapis tube of lipstick that Maccari had found under the sofa. He looked at it for a moment and held it out to the young woman.

"If you'll allow me… Look—this belongs to you."

The *contessina* took the little golden object. She polished it and asked him, "Where did you find this?"

"Here, on the floor in this room. It's an innocuous tube of lipstick… artificial cinnabar… lights up the face… a convention

121

and a concession. A sign of life, certainly, and you, signorina, you lost it here... you dropped it in this house."

After a brief silence he continued. "But it's not the only thing you lost last night in this house, Contessina..."

Maria Giovanna sighed painfully, as if to herself. "It's true! I also lost my wits here."

De Vincenzi approached her and said in a voice like a whisper, "And a phial of poison, which can rob you of your wits and your life!"

It hardly seemed possible, but Maria Giovanna went paler still. She almost felt dizzy. "How do you know?"

"Know? I didn't know the phial was yours. You, however, didn't think you had lost it."

The young woman wrung her hands in despair and moaned, "Oh, but this is torture!"

"Don't you want to tell me what really happened in here last night?"

He began pacing the room, still talking. "Sooner or later, I'll discover the whole truth... It's a closed circle, this. Closed within the walls of this apartment. Only a few people, and they are all in here. Shall I name them?"

Terrified, Maria Giovanna screamed, "I can't... I can't take any more!" And she fell back into her chair.

10

A Great Love

The inspector waited for some time for Maria Giovanna to calm down.

He watched her sobbing, her face in her hands, the tremors coming regularly. Her pain was terrible. He could have sworn her eyes were dry. They had to be dry and barren. It wasn't one of those babyish sobs, which free and cleanse one, but a real crisis of fear and anguish. Rebellion against something stronger, something cruel. A revolt against something that could no longer be avoided.

Under the brim of her black felt hat, a mass of blonde hair could be seen softly gathered at the nape of her neck, which was white and draped with gold.

De Vincenzi was still waiting.

Little by little her sobbing ceased and her shoulders stopped shaking. The young woman slowly revived and uncovered her face. Her large, deep-set eyes were pleading. She looked humbly at De Vincenzi, still standing in front of her.

"Why won't you believe me? Believe me, and stop questioning me—it's torture. Accept my confession!"

The inspector spoke quite gently to her. "Shall we try to find the truth together? The truth that you yourself are ignoring? Only when we've looked it squarely in the face will we be able to try to salvage whatever has not yet sunk to the bottom."

Maria Giovanna continued to look at him without speaking.

"As long as you would like to, Signorina Marchionni. For the love you feel for yourself, your father, for…"

He was about to mention Giannetto, but he stopped himself. The pale face of that other man had appeared to him, with its regular lines, slender and transparent as crystal… the man upstairs in the attic apartment, with all that furniture that was too nice for it.

Why not play that card now?

Time was of the essence. This wasn't the usual sort of investigation, to be conducted with bureaucratic plodding. Every minute was precious.

He looked at the door to the parlour, behind which the count must be waiting, and hesitated. Perhaps the old man was listening.

He shrugged. He knew that once everything was finished, once the truth was revealed, the ground would be seeded with ruin.

"For the love you feel for… Remigio Altieri." He pronounced it slowly, lowering his voice.

The young lady jumped to her feet, her face suddenly alight, her eyes flashing, her lips trembling with indignity.

"How dare you! Why do you mention that name?"

De Vincenzi attempted to calm her. He actually preferred her like this: ready to fight, and full of energy for it.

"Why did you mention him? Who gave you the right to root around in my life? How did you know?"

"You're forgetting that Remigio Altieri lives in the same building."

A light had gone on in his mind: "*la signorina*", as the porter's

124

wife and servant had called her, turned up almost every day in via Monforte, going by the lodge—but not always going to Aurigi.

"… and you don't want to recall that you came almost every day to visit him, up there, on the top floor…"

It was as if she'd collapsed. The blood that had risen to her cheeks now rushed back to her heart, leaving her face wan and white as marble.

"How did you know?" she whispered.

"It doesn't matter how I found out. The important thing is that Aurigi doesn't yet know anything."

And he pointed at the closed door to the dining room.

Maria Giovanna followed his gaze.

"Is he in there?" she asked, her voice a mere thread.

"In there, under arrest," the inspector stated firmly. "And perhaps he would prefer—"

"I'll tell him myself!" Maria Giovanna declared, stiffening. "I would have told him some time ago if—"

But she stopped.

"Well, none of this comes into it."

She had recovered her energy once more. De Vincenzi knew she would fight tooth and nail, like a tiger, now that her secret had been discovered. He would need to play it close now if he didn't want to forfeit his advantage.

But was his position really advantageous? Or had he lost his front? Wasn't he groping around again without having uncovered anything essential or concrete? Running here and there after ephemeral lights appearing in the shadows like the mythical, wind-blown will o' the wisp?

"Leave Remigio Altieri out of this for good!"

"For me that's not possible, Signorina Marchionni. Until I know who killed Garlini, it's impossible for me to exclude anyone. Signor Altieri must answer for himself, just like all the others."

"Oh no!" Her shout was muffled but nevertheless awful. There was such passion contained in it that shivers went right up the inspector's spine: he had the actual physical sensation of an intense electrical vibration.

How she loved him!

But why, then? How had she come to the point of accusing herself of having killed someone so as to save Giannetto?

She had actually been in the house that night. And she had lost a phial of poison, a tube of lipstick.

But she hadn't killed anyone. She couldn't have.

Why couldn't it have been her? the inspector asked himself once more. He shot a quick glance at the clock, the key to the mystery.

Maria Giovanna stood tall before the inspector, extremely proud, her flashing eyes fixed on him.

"Oh no!" she repeated. "You will not bring Remigio Altieri into all this. He has nothing to do with it. He is blameless apart from loving me, just as I love him. *Because I love him.* It would have taken something much greater and more powerful than our own love and our instinct for preservation for me to have ruined his life and mine. But I love him, don't you understand? I love no one but him! And perhaps by now I have indeed ruined his life! But to bring him into all this? No! Don't you understand that all this drama we're going through is despicable? And he is pure! He's above suspicion!"

She spoke rapidly but her voice remained quiet. She stopped and waited.

"Well, all this may be so," said De Vincenzi, *"but I must know."* He went to the door.

"Where are you going?" The young woman followed him and stood ready to fling herself in his way.

De Vincenzi did not turn around.

"Where are you going?" she repeated, and she took him by the arm.

"To his place." And, liberating himself from her grip, he continued walking. He opened the door.

"Stop! What do you want to know from him? I'll tell you everything—what there is to tell, that is… what I know… but don't question him. Don't let him know about this horrible thing. What do you think he can tell you?"

De Vincenzi stopped.

"Why did he come to live in this building?"

Maria Giovanna looked at him as if she were trying to read in his eyes just how much he already knew.

"But he didn't come here… he was here. I think he has always lived here."

"No. It's been barely two years."

"Oh!"

"Why do you keep lying?"

"But it's true. He came to live here when I got engaged to Giannetto Aurigi."

"So why did you get engaged to Aurigi if you didn't love him, and you loved someone else?"

The young woman hesitated. She didn't speak. Although she seemed confused, nothing about her betrayed shame or offended modesty.

Instead—a new anguish.

"Why are you doing this?" De Vincenzi insisted, acting the accuser. He stood with his hand on the latch, ready to open the door.

"I can't tell you that. *I can't tell you yet.* There was a reason and it was ironclad, terrible, gnawing, like divine punishment. But I can't reveal it. And allow me to hope that I'll never have to reveal it."

De Vincenzi said nothing. He watched her. She seemed sincere. And in any case, everything about her breathed such passion, such exclusive, almost violent love for the other man— the young man in the attic—that it was hard to imagine her yielding to renunciation without some formidable reason that was stronger than her or her ability to fight.

"Don't tell me. Perhaps it won't enter into all this. But it's a fact that when Remigio Altieri knew you had become engaged to someone else, a certain Giannetto Aurigi, he wanted to come and live in this building. Such was his level of feeling… or *the calculation* that pushed him to do this, and you to consent to it."

"Why are you talking about calculations?" the young woman exclaimed reproachfully. "I'd hoped you understood… that you were *human*…"

"I don't know. Why don't you explain it to me?"

"What do I need to explain? Altieri has been my French teacher since I was a young girl. Does that suggest he was too young himself? It's true! Papa preferred him to other professors… because… because he was less expensive… Papa has always been very careful with money."

She hurried over the last sentence, blushing, as if it were not the real reason and there was another.

She tried straightaway to brush it aside, skip over it.

128

"It was fate, I'm telling you! I could not have met him any other way. I had to meet him like that. And I loved him. Oh, not right away, naturally. In the first few years I didn't notice that he had feelings for me, or the ones that were bubbling up in my heart, day by day. He would never have dared to confess it to me, if one day... I must tell you that in the past few years, when I was already a young woman... a free signorina, or nearly, because my father has always given me a liberal education, and a sense of responsibility towards myself and others... very often Altieri and I took a walk during our lesson. As for the rest, it was only a matter of conversations in French, and not actual lessons. That day, around three years ago now, we had gone outside the city, beyond Acquabella. It was our favourite walk. A storm caught us out, one of those autumn downpours that break out suddenly and seem to drench the earth. We had gone beyond the railway line and we were in open countryside beyond the farms and houses. There was a bank with a ditch in it, the earth curved inwards down there to make a sort of vault... We ran to hide in that shelter. It was narrow, water was coming in sideways... We leant against each other, better than we could on the ground... and I found myself in his arms. It was like a flash of lightning! That embrace revealed me to myself. When we got back home, I knew I loved him."

She told him the story, reliving it in her memory, and so absorbed by it that she forgot the present realities. Her eyes shone, her cheeks burned.

"There you have it!" she said. And it really seemed to her that there was nothing more to be said. For her, everything began and ended with that love.

"And then?" the inspector asked gently. He too was moved and also, strangely upset somehow. He felt a great tenderness, an unexpected desire to do good, to sow happiness around him.

"And then?" he repeated. "Go on. I understand you."

"Yes," Maria Giovanna exclaimed, "perhaps you do understand me! But the rest is more difficult. I can't tell you everything. You must believe me, even if what I'm saying is unclear."

She gathered her thoughts for a moment.

De Vincenzi took his hand from the latch. It was now pointless to threaten her with going upstairs to see Remigio. Everything appeared to him to be so logical, so natural, *so good*.

"We had days of ecstasy. I felt as if I were in another world, as if I were no longer myself. Remigio came every day for my lesson... but now we had to talk about us, about our love. Remigio was making plans, and would have accepted any sacrifice. He would double his workload. He had to get to the point where he could find a position. I didn't, however, want to hide anything from my parents. I wanted them to know. Remigio told me the story of his father and I, too, felt I could abandon my family, flee with him as his mother had done... I didn't have the courage, though, to speak to Papa about it right away. But one morning my mamma questioned me. A mother misses nothing that's going on in her daughter's heart. I didn't know how to keep quiet, and I wouldn't lie to her, so I told her everything. My mamma adores me... I thought she'd open her arms to me, full of all the happiness I knew. But instead she burst into tears."

She paused and looked at De Vincenzi as if begging him to understand her and let her keep quiet about what she didn't want to say, or couldn't say.

"Yes. She burst into tears and told me my father wanted me to marry Giannetto Aurigi. I was crushed. My first instinct was to rebel. Apart from anything else, I didn't feel up to playing a part in some awful farce. But then…" She fell silent, her heart beating.

"What about Altieri?" asked De Vincenzi.

"Ah."

She moved away, went to the sofa and sat down, seemingly lost in thought. Trembling, she kept an eye on the dining room door.

Then she turned to face the inspector and spoke to him in a high voice, continuing her account without interruptions or gaps.

In her mind, unfortunately, there were no gaps.

"The first time I came to this building to visit Aurigi—I had to come here—I saw Remigio at the door. He was waiting for me. He told me he lived here, so I would always have him near. His suffering was boundless. He was a martyr, I'm telling you! It went on for two years, then a few days ago the horrible anguish of this drama was unleashed. And then last night's terrifying events… and then today… the awful present, which seems to me—"

"What drama?" asked the inspector, leaning towards the young woman. "What drama unfolded—"

"No!" she screamed. "No! I can't tell you! I mustn't!"

She stared at De Vincenzi, who kept coming closer to her, trying to read her mind through her eyes, and waved her hands in front of her as if to shoo him away.

"I'm the one who killed Garlini! I'm the one who killed him!"

She fell silent, in agony.

131

De Vincenzi moved away from her. He was annoyed and his face was tense.

Once again, he felt the truth escaping him.

That story had only served to distract him from the crucial point of his investigation. And it had allowed the young woman to recover and to entrench herself behind her heroic and pointless lie.

Ah, no! He would get to the bottom of this.

Her youth, already tormented by suffering, pained him. But someone had died. He had a duty, and there was also the absolute necessity—which he'd taken upon himself—of saving Aurigi. All the more so now that he knew Aurigi to be unhappy, his masculinity impugned, his heart wounded.

Everything she'd told him was probably genuine. In fact, he considered it to be true and sincere. But it didn't explain the murder, it didn't explain her presence in the apartment on the very night of the crime; and, above all, it didn't explain the phial of poison.

And then there was the other person, all the way upstairs. Someone whose existence suddenly seemed to throw a glaring light on events. Someone who must know something—since how could he have slept easy while, only a short way away, the woman he loved was involved in a cruel tragedy?

He would take action.

He looked at the woman. Of course! He would begin with her.

11

Pain Beyond Pain

The parlour door opened and Count Marchionni appeared on the threshold.

His face was tense, his eyes flashing. With trembling lips, he stood silently watching his daughter and De Vincenzi. Both were seeing this horrible incident through to the end.

After the briefest of pauses, De Vincenzi said decisively, "Well then, signorina, I'll talk about it. But it will be more painful for you, because I'll have to resort to logic rather than fantasy in order to reconstruct the tormented workings of the brain. And it will be brutal, because I've had to hunt for the truth, looking into things and beyond appearances."

Marchionni took a step forward to intervene. His voice was cutting. "Appearances can be deceptive, Inspector!"

De Vincenzi calmly turned round and asked bitterly, "Do you want to hear?"

"You are proceeding in an irregular manner. What value can there be in a confession extorted from a woman by your methods?"

The remark hit the inspector like a blow to the chest. He flinched, and the blood rushed to his cheeks. He hurried towards the dining room door.

"Well, if you want it like that, we'll do things the regular way." He knocked at the door. "Open up! It's me, the inspector."

The door opened immediately and the officer appeared. De Vincenzi shoved him aside roughly.

"Go! Go over there… into that room… wherever you like." He pushed him towards the entrance hallway, closed the door behind him and rapidly retraced his steps.

"Aurigi! Aurigi! Come here."

Giannetto appeared, still in evening dress, his face tired, his look dazed. As soon as he saw Maria Giovanna and the count, he moved away from them in an effort to defend himself. He backed off, but De Vincenzi made him stay.

"No! Come in." He pushed Aurigi to the centre of the room and looked at the count as if in challenge.

"There you go, we're almost all here. Do you consider the proceedings to be regular now, Count Marchionni?"

"I don't think so!" the old man declared. "I've heard about the investigating magistrate and I know the penal code."

De Vincenzi immediately replied, with some irony, "And do you also know Tardieu's classic tract on the symptoms and course of prussic acid poisoning?"

"What are you going on about?" asked the count.

Maria Giovanna leapt forward and cried in a petrified voice, "No! Not that—you have no right!"

But De Vincenzi didn't hold back.

"I'm saying"—his tone was icy—"and I have every right to say, Count, that last night your daughter dropped a phial in this house which had enough prussic acid in it to kill half a dozen people."

"Were you here last night?" the count yelled at Maria Giovanna. But it was a desperate plea more than anything else.

"She was here," said De Vincenzi, interposing himself between father and daughter, "*while you were at the Savini or the Clubino.*"

The count and the inspector confronted one another.

"How can you deny it if your daughter admits it?"

The other man replied sarcastically, "She also confessed to having killed Garlini!"

"Absolutely. And yet she did not kill him. We can agree on that. But what makes you certain, Count, that she did not kill him?"

Marchionni hesitated very briefly before shrugging. "She wouldn't have been able to."

"Why don't you also say that she had no motive for killing him?"

"What motive could she have had?"

"I asked you!"

"Only one person had any interest in killing Garlini."

"Is that what you think?"

"Him!"

"As a matter of fact," De Vincenzi resumed with some force, "Aurigi, too, has admitted to killing him. Don't you think two confessions of guilt for one crime are too many? And doesn't it seem that your implacable desire to accuse Aurigi is… inexplicable?"

"My daughter is melodramatically sacrificing herself for a noble love."

"Do you really think so? In any case, the sacrifice was pointless."

The two men's discussion unfolded quickly, and Aurigi now addressed Maria Giovanna in a shaken voice.

"But why? Why? Why did you want to do this? Why did they bring you here?"

The young girl got up, so pale she was trembling. She staggered, answering as if in a trance, her words like those of a sleepwalker. All her conscious effort was focused on containing her inner turmoil.

"Giannetto! Giannetto, I'm about to behave very cowardly towards you—by speaking up too late. If I'd spoken to you earlier, perhaps none of this would have happened."

De Vincenzi instinctively moved away. This drama, he knew, was moving like a living thing, and had passed into the hands of these two individuals tossed about by destiny. For a short time he could do nothing but watch. But he understood things well enough to listen from a distance, his soul in his eyes.

Marchionni wanted to intervene, but he couldn't, restrained by a force beyond his control. He sensed that something new, different, even worse was about to happen.

"What do you mean, Maria Giovanna?" Aurigi asked in terror.

When the answer came, it was terrible.

"I don't love you, Giannetto! I have never loved you. I have always considered you only a friend... a good friend."

Aurigi, already physically exhausted, did not immediately take in the meaning of her words. Like a whining child, he asked plaintively, "Why are you saying this, Maria Giovanna? Do you, too, feel the need to renounce the past now?"

"No. Have you asked yourself why I'm here? Well, I'll tell you. I came because remorse drove me here. Remorse for having induced you to do what you did."

Aurigi wrung his hands, as if to banish an obsessional vision.

He went towards Maria Giovanna and was about to shout when he noticed De Vincenzi and Marchionni. He kept quiet.

The young woman continued.

"Remorse for never having loved you and for letting you believe that I did… and for having misled you. It's the truth, Giannetto. I was going to marry you only because you are rich… *because I thought you were rich*… and my father needed a rich man to help him."

The count clenched his fists. "Maria Giovanna, I forbid you!" he hissed.

Maria Giovanna threw her head back. The more humiliated she felt as a result of her confession, the straighter and taller she stood.

"What would you like to forbid me, Papa? I cannot remain quiet, I can no longer keep quiet! Do you think it won't come out tomorrow? Now… Oh! No, they're going through our lives… right into the depths of our souls… I would have preferred to keep quiet, too, I did for some time. But I see now that it is no longer possible to hide the truth."

She faced Aurigi once more.

"Our family's situation was precarious. A beautiful façade, and behind it ruins. A palazzo, servants, but the weight of the daily struggle to prop up this semblance of wealth nearly crushed us."

She went on, concealing nothing and overwhelmed by the pangs of the horrible confession she was making to Aurigi, whom she'd deceived and who she believed she'd driven to murder.

"Until a few years ago, I ignored the tragic and heroic struggle my mother and father were making: land sold off here and there, economies… silver, pictures, expensive furniture, all sold off far from here and replaced with silver-plated brass and copies. Then came the time for my mother's jewels to go, then debts."

She turned, pointing to her father, but there was nothing of the accuser about her.

"He's struggled with a courage I admire. He hid everything from me, he's always hidden it. And now he's suffering even more because he knows I know. My mother had to confess it all to me. She told me I was my father's only hope! Nothing but a good marriage could save us—*my* good marriage. And so, since they thought you were rich, Giannetto, since they told me that only you could save us, I consented to marry you… I became your fiancée."

She'd said everything, but she added with a sob, "Only… only I hadn't reflected that you actually really loved me and that sooner or later the moment would come when I would have to make this horrible confession to you."

Stooped under the weight of her words, the count heard Maria Giovanna out. When a sob interrupted her sentence, he suddenly found the strength to react.

"Enough! Enough! Not a single word of what this crazy girl has said is true. As proof, there's the sheer fact of the state in which Aurigi finds himself. Had I wanted a rich son-in-law, I wouldn't have chosen him!"

Another silence followed—full of anxiety.

Maria Giovanna made a move towards her father. Tenderly, as if she were trying to convince him, she said, "Are you trying to say that he tricked you, Papa? That you've been hoodwinked? Yes, that's true. We did believe Aurigi was rich; perhaps he himself did everything he could to make us believe it. But I feel as responsible as Giannetto for what happened in this house last night. That's why I came here. It wasn't right for me to abandon him; I couldn't do it. I didn't love him and I don't love him, but he believed in my love to the extent that he'd have killed so as not to lose me."

Giannetto practically leapt at Maria Giovanna. He was livid, his face tense, his muscles pulsing as he struggled to contain the explosive violence of his passion. He grabbed her wrist and the voice that issued from him was inhuman, a hateful hiss.

"How do you know I'm the killer? How can you say that? Even at this very moment you're playing some sort of hellish comedy in order to get rid of me! You slu—"

De Vincenzi watched the miserable argument between two absolutely desperate souls with detachment. Now he came up behind them. Conscious that Giannetto could no longer control himself, he took his arm and squeezed it so hard that Giannetto was forced to let go of Maria Giovanna's wrist.

"Quiet! Be quiet, Giannetto."

Violently, he pushed Aurigi as far away as he could.

"Quiet!"

When he saw Giannetto leaning against the wall, his eyes dull, his mouth suddenly downturned, he turned to Maria Giovanna and caught her just as she was about to faint. He gently led her to the sofa and made her sit down.

Silence fell over the room once more.

De Vincenzi was always the first to break it.

Leaning over Maria Giovanna, he spoke tenderly, "Last night, Contessina Maria Giovanna, you were in this house."

The young woman bent her head.

"Why were you here? You must tell me everything now."

But Marchionni intervened decisively.

"*I* will speak, Inspector!"

"No. Not yet," said De Vincenzi, his voice anxious. "The moment will come for you to speak, Count Marchionni. But it's not now."

"But it's my right, by God!"

"No! I'm telling you, only one man here in this room just now has the right to question, and that's me. A crime has been committed, let's not forget that. Though there may be other details surrounding this decisive fact, which have moved the wheels of social justice, other personal tragedies that to each of you may seem fundamental, or for each one of you seem the central fact, I must concern myself only with the crime and its author. Anything else matters to me only in so far as it illuminates the situation. You must keep quiet now, Count Marchionni, or I shall be obliged to escort you elsewhere."

Marchionni shut up.

The inspector turned once more to Maria Giovanna. His voice was steady. "Contessina, you dropped a tube of lipstick in this room and a phial of prussic acid over there, in the bathroom. How I could ascertain that it was you who dropped the phial, I didn't know. It could have been you or someone else. What I'm saying is that I had no proof. I immediately guessed it, but I had no proof until you yourself confessed to me. And now I know it was you. Therefore, you were here last night. You didn't kill Garlini, but you were here. Do you want to tell me how and why?"

Maria Giovanna raised her eyes to De Vincenzi, and in them he read a desperate plea.

He answered her look. "Yes, yes, it's both necessary and essential. Anything that can still be saved will be saved only if you speak."

The young woman said with a sigh, "I came here to meet Garlini."

"You knew that Garlini would be here in this house at midnight?"

"Yes."

De Vincenzi was about to ask another question, but he looked at Giannetto and hesitated. Then he made up his mind.

"Did Garlini know you were coming?"

Aurigi jumped to his feet. "No! What are you saying? Maria Giovanna knew about Garlini through me. She'd noticed that I'd been worried and agitated for several days, that I was seriously distressed. In a moment of excitement last night at the theatre, not knowing how I was going to pay Garlini more than a half million, I told her everything… my situation… the appointment with Garlini at my house… the time, and that I would have to pay Garlini the total that night. I got him to wait until midnight, although he wanted the payment yesterday afternoon. Seeing my ruin as inevitable, I confessed to Maria Giovanna in a moment of weakness that I'd asked Garlini to come to my house at midnight in order to—"

His voice broke down and it was De Vincenzi who continued coldly, "Keep going! To kill him. Keep going."

"Yes," said Aurigi. "I wrote him a note that afternoon, telling him I was counting on his promise to wait until that night, and telling him to come, because I was ready to honour my obligation and pay him the sum. Garlini had to file the end-of-the-month balance yesterday, and if my overdraft had appeared on it I would have been ruined, so I wanted to ensure that he would hide it. I was ready for anything." With a grimace, he said: "Even to kill him… but not in here, naturally, I'm not such an idiot! I would have done it outside. There you have it."

De Vincenzi stood in front of him, looking him straight in the face.

"And Signorina Maria Giovanna knew this?"

"Yes. My nerves were shot, I had a moment of weakness. In the afternoon there'd been a terrible scene with him—with Count Marchionni. At La Scala, I lost control of myself when Maria Giovanna questioned me. I told her everything and then fled the theatre… and came here."

The inspector summed it up in a frosty voice. "However, you did not kill him."

"It was too late! I never carry a watch. I thought it wasn't even eleven-thirty, and yet I got here and saw by the pendulum clock over there that it was half past midnight. There was no one in the house. I thought Garlini had been and gone, after ringing the bell futilely. I waited until a quarter to one, and then I left. I thought I was going crazy. I walked around the city without knowing where I was going… I felt like the cold was doing me good, but I was suddenly overcome by mortal exhaustion. I needed to think about nothing, to sleep, to forget, to erase myself. So I came to see you at the police station. I had no idea where to go at that hour. I was afraid of going back home, afraid of being by myself. In the back of my mind, I thought you would protect me if I were near you, and I wouldn't kill anyone. I can't explain it to you, but that's how it was."

He spoke rapidly, as if to empty his entire being, to bare his soul through confession. And then he stopped speaking, completely worn down.

De Vincenzi slowly turned towards Maria Giovanna and then towards the count. They were silent. Amazed, they had heard Giannetto out with horrified astonishment painted all over their faces.

They looked at De Vincenzi, fearing he was about to make a frightening accusation. If Giannetto wasn't the killer, who was it? Then Maria Giovanna's father turned to study her. She didn't dare look at him.

With the same slowness, De Vincenzi now twisted round to look at the pendulum clock.

"You saw the time there on that clock, which was showing half past midnight, while it was actually eleven-thirty. In the same way that it's now a quarter past ten and the clock shows an hour later. Yes, that's how it is."

He swiftly changed tack, and his voice changed too, as if he didn't want the others to grasp the mystery of the clock that was running an hour fast.

"And you, why did you come here? What did you have in mind?" he asked the Contessina Marchionni.

It was time for confessions.

The nerves of those three people were exposed, and as taut as the strings on a violin. Not one of them could have kept quiet, or lied.

Maria Giovanna spoke. "I found myself in this house yesterday afternoon while Aurigi was meeting with my father. I heard everything: that Aurigi was ruined, that he'd have to repay an enormous sum that night. I realized that our ruin would accompany Aurigi's. My father's words to Giannetto were clear to me. He, too, was at desperation point. His only hope, I knew, lay in my marriage… and I had unexpectedly

143

learnt that Aurigi was ruined! So I left. I took a taxi and I went to see Garlini."

Aurigi's bellow was desperate.

"No!"

"Yes," the young woman answered, and she continued quietly. "Garlini had been courting me for some time. I thought he was a gentleman, believed he was really in love with me. I hoped to have some influence on him and instead I discovered—Oh!"

A deep shiver ran through Maria Giovanna. She covered her face with her hands, murmuring, "How disgusting!"

But she collected herself straightaway and, uncovering her face, she spoke coldly and with incredible bitterness.

"His look spoke louder than his words. He told me that Aurigi had promised to repay him that night, but he didn't believe he would. He was determined to ruin him. He had offered him very high credit precisely so that he'd be left with no escape route. He knew that sooner or later I would have to come to him and yield to him if I wanted to save myself from scandal. He had me watch him write the repayment down in his accounts book, as if Aurigi had made it already. He said to me, 'Well, if he doesn't pay me tonight, Contessina, you will! I'll wait until eleven at my house tomorrow. If you don't come, I'll ruin Aurigi.' He prepared a receipt for Giannetto, sneering, 'Here's the receipt. I'm giving it to you, not to him.'"

Maria Giovanna fell silent, exhausted.

There was a long pause.

Giannetto had fallen back into his chair and was staring into space.

Maria Giovanna's father was suffering, and suffering so intensely that his eyes seemed nearly crazed with pain.

Gently, De Vincenzi asked, "And then? And then you went to the hospital, is that right, Contessina?"

"Yes, but how did you know?"

"You are pursuing a nursing course at the Red Cross. You went to the hospital pharmacy and you took the phial of prussic acid."

"Yes!" shouted Maria Giovanna, interrupting him. "I could not have survived the shame. And I had to save my family from ruin! Giannetto... Giannetto had gambled on my father's behalf as well, and my father couldn't pay. It's the truth, and I learnt it yesterday afternoon while I was hiding just there, in that room, while Giannetto and my father were arguing. It's the truth, and Aurigi has even now been generous to the point of continuing to conceal it."

De Vincenzi turned to the count.

"Is it the truth?"

With obvious effort but in a clear voice, Marchionni answered, "Yes, it's the truth."

"So last night," the inspector began again straightaway, facing Maria Giovanna, "when you learnt that Aurigi was ready to kill in order to save you and your father, you came here to prevent it and... to succumb to Garlini?"

"Yes. And I would have killed myself afterwards."

"But instead?"

Clearly struggling to control herself, the young woman continued.

"I arrived after midnight. I couldn't get away before then because I had to go through the farce of visiting another box at the theatre to see some friends so my father and mother wouldn't know. And I found Garlini dead."

"The door was open?" asked De Vincenzi.

"The main entrance down below was open, and the one to this apartment was half open. I came in… and there inside, in the parlour… the body."

She covered her face with her hands, overcome by horror.

But the inspector would not give her a break.

"And you immediately fled?"

"I was so frightened," Maria Giovanna continued, taking her hands from her face. "And my remorse was horrendous—for having arrived too late, for having been unable to prevent the frightful act! I could not bear the strain. When I heard someone come in—there, through that door—an insane fear came over me. I escaped, through there, at the back, into the bathroom. It was dark, I tripped over the chairs, my purse fell out of my hand—that's how I must have lost the phial. And I stayed in there, shocked, holding my breath, until—"

She hesitated. Stopped speaking.

Count Marchionni continued. "Until I turned on the light and saw her there and helped her up and took her home. There you have it! Now you know everything. Even that I was here last night, that I knew about Aurigi's appointment and also, naturally, about my daughter. That I, too, could have killed Garlini and did not. I did not kill him. Do you understand, Inspector?"

After a silence, the count's voice was heard again. This time he was sarcastic.

"So now that you know everything, if it wasn't one of us who killed him, *who was it*?"

146

12

Darkness

And in fact, now that the three principal protagonists in this dismal sequence of events had been eliminated, the darkness was thicker than ever.

If not one of those three—that is, Giannetto, Maria Giovanna or Count Marchionni—then who?

The inspector had not responded to the count's question. But he felt in himself that those three had surely told the truth, and that would be worth less than nothing if it were not corroborated by evidence.

My personal conviction is worthless if I don't succeed in finding the person guilty of murder, De Vincenzi thought, and he said to himself anxiously, I must find him immediately, before the investigating magistrate comes back and acts. In these few rooms there is enough evidence against Maria Giovanna and her father to justify the immediate arrest of all three of them, certainly to condemn them all as well. If the affair goes to the investigating magistrate, I can't do anything, because my intuition and my psychological impressions will have no weight. They'll be caught in a machine that will grind them up. Since I know they're innocent of the crime, I must attempt the impossible to save them!

Yet none of these reflections was keeping him from fumbling around in the dark in trying to solve the murder of Garlini.

The clock that ran an hour ahead had been the first glimmer of light for him. But it hadn't served only to convince him of the innocence of those three. If the clock had been put forward by an hour, it was undoubtedly connected with the crime. Whoever had taken the trouble to move the hands forward must have had a clear objective.

De Vincenzi had understood that from the beginning, and what's more, he'd realized it couldn't have been Giannetto, or Maria Giovanna, or her father.

If it had been committed by one of those three, the crime could only have been one of passion: hate, and the unleashing of someone's bloodlust. Someone with their back to the wall, confronted with ruin.

If Giannetto were the killer, the crime might have been premeditated, or certainly a desperate act. It would have been strange for him to have killed Garlini in his own house. This was precisely what had perplexed the inspector from the beginning. It could have happened that way, and yet the rest of Giannetto's confession had confirmed that he had wanted Garlini to come to his own house so that he could kill him somewhere else— and he was then forced by circumstances to change his plan and to rush things.

In any event, it was inexplicable in each case that the clock's hands should have been put forward.

Maria Giovanna or the elderly count could have killed Garlini for more complex but nevertheless similar motives. Now De Vincenzi had it from the mouths of these two unfortunate people that at least one of them had had it in mind to eliminate the man—and then he or she had been confronted with the accomplished deed.

That man, the father, would almost certainly have been capable of carrying out his intentions; but then surely the crime would have been framed differently, and the clues and trails would have spoken for themselves.

Above all, the clue of the pendulum clock would not have existed, *because it couldn't have*. How could the count have put the hands forward by an hour, and why would he have done so?

That was it! This objection was enough to make an intelligent and observant man such as De Vincenzi immediately eliminate those three figures from the picture. But it was not yet enough to indicate the killer, and even less to constitute such dazzling proof as to lift all suspicion from the suspects.

De Vincenzi pondered all this with detachment, turning it over in his mind, and his face reflected the effort of his brain.

The three people surrounding him were full of anxiety, since they could guess what was passing through the inspector's head.

Both Maria Giovanna and Marchionni had to face the fact—new to them—of Giannetto's innocence. When they'd found Garlini's body in Aurigi's house, they'd both told themselves that the killer could be only one person.

Maria Giovanna still had the sound of Giannetto's raised voice in her ears, and as for the count, he knew Aurigi's desperation all too well to doubt that it had been he. All the more so since he carried that same desperation in his own heart, and it had brought him the same terrible consequences.

But now they had learnt that Giannetto hadn't killed anyone. And they had immediately said to themselves that with Giannetto out of the picture, suspicion would logically fall on them.

Marchionni's concern to justify his own and his daughter's presence in the house just before the crime had already pushed him into hiring the services of a private detective, someone who would follow the investigation and discover the culprit, the person considered to be the true author of the crime.

Marchionni was afraid. Not for himself, but for his daughter. As for Maria Giovanna, she was simply shocked. She couldn't think of anything other than the complete ruin of her life—and about Remigio, who was lost to her for ever.

As for Giannetto, the third actor in the drama, he had to add the terrible pain of Maria Giovanna's revelation to all the anguish of the day and the horrendous torments of the previous night, when he'd believed Garlini wouldn't come to his house and that his own ruin was inevitable. He was now stretched out in the armchair he had sat down in, his body unmoving, his eyes staring ahead at nothing.

He had loved Maria Giovanna. He had perhaps loved her poorly, in the way of a man who wants to live freely and independently, who is secure in himself and accustomed to using women solely for pleasure or to gratify his senses: the aesthetic as well as the rougher, more instinctual one.

But there was no doubt that he'd harboured great tenderness for her and had been ready to kill Garlini to save her, above all, from ruin.

And all at once he'd learnt that she did not love him. That she'd never loved him.

A horrible feeling of emptiness engulfed him. In his mouth was the bitter taste of a cruel pain. His lips were set firmer and deeper, as if he were grimacing.

The silence persisted for several moments.

Marchionni's sarcastic utterance had effectively raised a barrier in front of each of them. If not one of those three, then who had it been?

De Vincenzi shook himself.

"It's necessary to act now. And only I can do so," he said in a firm voice.

He looked each of them in the face, adding, "There's nothing else for you to do. My personal conviction has no value. I believe in the statements you've offered, but that won't stop the investigating magistrate from proceeding against you. If he doesn't find the real culprit, not one of you three has much hope of getting out of this."

Aurigi interrupted him, and the sneer on his lips was accentuated by a frightening smile.

"Well, if you're worried about me, you can save yourself the trouble. Nothing has any further importance for me."

He threw a quick glance at Maria Giovanna and concluded, "No, I mean it. I'm not interested in anything that happens to me!"

De Vincenzi understood him perfectly well, but he had to react, and he did so somewhat violently.

"Ah, my dear friend, you're not the only one in this. There's Signorina Maria Giovanna, who is just as compromised as you are. There's her father. And above all, there's an interest in human justice, which I believe in and which I must uphold this time."

He paused for a moment before adding coldly, "Personal tragedies can sometimes become a luxury one cannot allow. I must solve this problem and I have no time to lose. I must ask that you, as well as the others, apply yourself to helping me. And Giannetto, you'll do it."

Aurigi had been listening. He gestured vaguely.

"Well?" he asked diffidently.

"Well, I want to try to solve the problem before this evening. I may not succeed. But then chance, which I believe in, may help me."

He made for the door at the back of the room and pulled it open.

Giacomo was in the hallway, apparently intent on dusting the furniture.

The inspector pretended not to notice him and went to the telephone.

He called the king's prosecutor and fell into conversation with the investigating magistrate. He knew him only by name and by sight.

As for the investigating magistrate, he had no idea who De Vincenzi was—or affected not to know, displaying all the studied indifference with which investigating magistrates treat police officers. He immediately informed De Vincenzi that he would return to the scene of the crime within the hour.

De Vincenzi had to employ all his powers of persuasion to get him to agree to postpone the visit until four. "At that hour," he promised, "I'll have news."

The other man was incredulous. "What sort of news? The way things appeared this morning, it's all so clear and simple that I can't imagine what news you could have in store for me."

De Vincenzi didn't want to commit himself, but the investigating magistrate insisted on having some formal assurance.

"It's not possible for me to explain by phone, sir," he concluded with some impatience. "I'm only asking you to give me a free hand until four."

The investigating magistrate, although unenthusiastic, postponed the search and the questioning, "but only to appease you".

De Vincenzi's face was dark as he put down the receiver.

The man would certainly never excuse error or delay. He had his mind properly made up and it was easy to guess what he thought: he must have had the warrant ready for Aurigi's arrest.

He turned and saw the bent back of the servant, who was busier than ever dusting the chest. He stared at him briefly before rapidly returning to the drawing room.

The others were waiting for him. Maria Giovanna and Count Marchionni were clearly worried.

Giannetto barely lifted his head when De Vincenzi entered. His was a look of tired discouragement. The look of an injured dog who watches his master getting all worked up about his care, knowing perfectly well that the effort is wasted. At least they might let me die in peace, it said. The inspector understood his pain and avoided his eyes.

"I need a few hours by myself," he said. "It's necessary for me to be able to do things my own way. Count, you can go back home with your daughter. I ask you to come back here again, to this house, at three-thirty."

The count bowed. "Do you think you'll manage to find the killer?"

"I hope so," the inspector answered.

Maria Giovanna followed her father, who was walking towards the door. But when she got to the threshold of the drawing room, she quickly turned back.

"Will you promise not to tell him anything?" she whispered with a pang.

"I promise you I won't tell him anything he doesn't need to know," De Vincenzi responded evasively.

He pushed her gently towards the door and warned her when she got there, "Don't even try to see him until four. My officers will keep you away."

The young woman descended the stairs, her head drooping as though crushed by an enormous weight.

"You stay here," De Vincenzi said to Giannetto. "I'll have to leave an officer in the house, of course."

Aurigi nodded apathetically.

The inspector let in the officer who'd been standing guard on the landing. He took him into the parlour, closed the door and spoke to him quietly. The officer listened to him attentively, every now and again muttering, "Got it, sir."

But he probably understood little or nothing. De Vincenzi's words had obviously astonished him.

When his superior had finished talking, he asked hesitatingly, "So you believe that?"

"I believe nothing," the inspector answered coldly. "And I ask you not to believe anything either."

He left in a hurry. He made as if to go downstairs, and when he was sure the officer had closed the door, he quickly went back up to the top floor.

Remigio opened the door and ushered him in with a sad, resigned smile.

"Make yourself comfortable," he said. "I thought you would be back soon. And so? Have you found out?"

The inspector didn't answer.

He sat down at the table and the other man sat across from him. They looked at each other for several moments.

A handsome young man, thought De Vincenzi. He probably didn't deserve everything that was happening to him. Why just like his father? The same fate! It made one believe it wasn't only individuals, but families, too, who were marked, one generation after another. What had happened twenty years before was repeating itself, this time with the small complication of a body mixed up in it all.

"Why didn't you tell me you went out last night?" the inspector asked at once, looking sharply at Remigio and enunciating every syllable.

The young man was shaken. He had expected something entirely different.

"What does that have to do with anything?" he asked. "You didn't ask me about it."

"Actually, I specifically asked you where you had been last night between twelve and one."

"Maybe. But it didn't occur to me that you'd be very interested in knowing that I went out for a walk at around one."

"At several degrees below zero? In the fog?"

"I was out of cigarettes."

"Where did you go to buy them?"

"See? Not even that can help you. I got them from a machine on the side of the Duomo, in front of the Rinascente department store. And the machine can't testify!"

"True. So, you went out at one; did you come back home?"

"Well, a little later... I was probably out about twenty minutes at most. As you've said, with that cold and fog it wasn't really the time to take a walk through the park."

"Or to Acquabella."

The young man jumped.

"Why do you say that?"

"Are you sure you didn't meet up last night, during your nocturnal walk… with the Contessina Marchionni?"

"What are you saying?! You're joking or delirious. But if it's a joke, it is in the worst taste."

His voice trembled as he spoke. It was clear that he was prepared for anything on his own territory.

"As it happens, I have no desire to make jokes. Signorina Marchionni was in this building last night."

The young man now paled. He couldn't speak for several moments.

"Are you sure of that?" he asked with contained desperation.

"Why are you so afraid that I'm sure of it?"

"Because it's unbelievable!"

Silence hung over the room.

De Vincenzi waited for the other man to recover himself, and then stated, "And in this building, last night, a man was killed."

The young man jumped to his feet but had to lean against the table when his legs gave way.

"What! Why are you insinuating such a thing? Do you know whom you're speaking about?"

"I'm not saying or insinuating anything. Sit down. It's better if we discuss this calmly."

Remigio turned and fell heavily into his chair. Terrified, he looked at the inspector.

"Tell me everything! I beg you: tell me everything!"

"I can't tell you any more than I already have. You, however, *can and must* tell me everything."

156

"I don't know anything!"

"Why did you go out at one?"

"For cigarettes."

"One doesn't go out at that hour to buy cigarettes."

"If one has a vice like mine, one does worse."

"In any case, if you went out at one, you couldn't have avoided meeting someone on the stairs."

The young man hesitated, but only momentarily.

"I didn't go out at one. I lied to you, and I don't even know why myself. Maybe I unconsciously accepted your suggestion about the time. It would have been midnight... maybe a few minutes before."

"And you met no one?"

"Yes... someone appeared... in front of me... below the second floor... a man was going downstairs... I only saw his back, because he walked faster when he heard my step."

"You didn't recognize him?"

"No. He was wearing a grey hat and a long, dark overcoat."

"Ah. And Aurigi's door... Signor Aurigi's door was open?"

Remigio struck his forehead with the palm of his hand.

"It's coming back to me now! It must have been half open, I had the idea that it was open without really noticing it for sure. When I go past that door, I avert my gaze."

"So you went out at midnight. And then?"

"And then? Nothing. I went to the Piazza del Duomo, I really did buy cigarettes and I came back home."

"And did you find the main door closed?"

"Open. But that often happens. The main door of this building is almost always open."

"Hmm," De Vincenzi reflected.

So this man too had left his attic room at precisely the moment when someone was murdering or had only just murdered Garlini. He too was in the vicinity of the bloody apartment and he too had a close relationship with one of the principal protagonists in this matter—still as dark and tangled as the moment when Maccari's calm voice had announced to him that a body had been found at 45 via Monforte.

De Vincenzi had, without a doubt, discovered many things. All the same, they had convinced him deep down that Aurigi had not killed, and neither had Maria Giovanna or Count Marchionni.

Who, then?

He was proceeding by elimination. It was a method that only appeared foolproof: let himself be swayed by some poorly observed fact or—even worse—by his own secret conviction, and he'd commit an error from which there'd be no going back.

Only a few suspects now remained if this drama had come full circle. Perhaps two, maybe only one.

The young man in front of him was completely consumed by romantic passion. De Vincenzi saw it in his face and in his eyes, which settled now and again on the portrait of Maria Giovanna, shining on it feverishly.

How far would he have gone for his love?

He had already acted strangely by going to live in the same building as Aurigi. Why had he done that? Out of some sort of cruel and self-destructive need to be near the man who was ruining his life? To stand as a constant and living image of reproof for the girl who'd strangled the pure and noble love in his heart, who'd bent to her duties as a daughter and perhaps to some atavistic law of obedience, the cast-iron demands of her class?

Or had he had a plan—simultaneously crazy, desperate and premeditated?

But then, how did he suddenly find himself in the thick of this drama involving three souls and the banker Garlini with his forty million?

Was it really possible that this young man—seemingly so loyal, with soft, clear eyes and broad, bright forehead—had in him such subtle wickedness as to conceive this monstrous crime, so that suspicion should fall on his rival and eliminate him? Certainly his skills, those of an accomplished criminal, could be considered truly diabolical if he'd preferred that roundabout way of getting rid of Aurigi to a direct attempt on the person of Maria Giovanna's fiancé—one that would have been much more dangerous for him.

In the latter case, suspicion would immediately fall on the young inhabitant of the attic rooms. However, the other way…

De Vincenzi thought about all of this while he continued to observe Remigio Altieri.

Remigio appeared to be lost in thought. His eyes flashed with terror. The effort he was making to avoid looking at Maria Giovanna's portrait was obvious—as if he were afraid of it, or ashamed.

All at once, the inspector got up with a movement so sudden and determined that Altieri was startled. He looked at him anxiously.

De Vincenzi seemed to be trying to react against himself by making a definitive decision.

"So, you don't want to tell me anything else?"

"What could I tell you?"

The inspector stood at the door. He asked casually, "When did you last see Maria Giovanna?"

Caught by surprise, Remigio spluttered, "Yesterday…"

"Afternoon?"

"Yes."

"What time?"

"It would have been about five… five-thirty… I don't know."

"Where?"

The young man's hesitation changed to obvious embarrassment. He murmured, "But why… why do you want to know it from me?" and his supplicating tone was distressing to hear.

De Vincenzi stood at the door, blocking it.

"I'll tell you when you saw her. It was at five, and she was leaving this building, almost running."

"Well, if you already know!" the other exclaimed.

"Did you see her take a taxi?"

"Yes."

"And you followed her!" the inspector's voice was sharp and insistent.

But Altieri shouted, "No! No! I did not! I did not do that!"

Exhausted, his nerves aching, with no more strength or control, he burst into convulsive sobs.

De Vincenzi closed the door and went downstairs.

13

Trial and Error

De Vincenzi found Cruni waiting for him at the police station.

"I did everything you asked me to, sir," the sergeant told him. He approached De Vincenzi with a triumphant air.

The inspector looked at him.

"Count Marchionni did not go to the Clubino or to the Savini last night."

"So?" the inspector asked indifferently.

Cruni was stupefied. After all the orders he'd been given, he couldn't account for this apathy.

"Oh, I was very careful, you can be sure of that. But at the Clubino every member has to sign the register when entering or leaving, and it was easy for me to consult it without giving the doorman a reason. As for the Savini, all the waiters know the count and all I had to do was question them like nothing was going on to discover the truth."

"And?"

"Ah! Do you want to know when he got back to his palazzo? It must have been two. He went back in a taxi along with his daughter. The signorina seemed to be suffering—the doorman told me—I knew how to get it out of him, right? That one won't speak, for sure… Now we know for a fact that the count lied."

"I know," De Vincenzi said nonchalantly, going to sit down at his table.

"You know?" the sergeant exclaimed, eyes wide. "So, I…"

"You carried out your duty scrupulously, dear Cruni, and I thank you. Only this is old news now. Events are moving along, my friend."

"Did you find out something?"

"I haven't found out anything."

He pushed his papers around. He came across the two volumes he'd been reading the night before when Aurigi had come in, and he sighed… if he could only go back to his books and not bother himself further with all these crimes! Now he understood what Maccari had been saying. At that moment, he too wished he could retreat to the country; at least Maccari had quickly sloughed off the bother of these awful events. Yet he himself could not *and must not*.

He thought about Giannetto, about Maria Giovanna and about that other unfortunate man, crying in his room on the top floor.

Once more he heard the investigating magistrate's ironic tone: *What sort of news do you think you'll have?*

Well, what news *did* he have, and what would he say to him in just a short while—at four o'clock?

He looked at the clock. It was two. He'd had a quick bite while he was at the Monumentale. He knew the bullet that had killed Garlini had been shot from the revolver found in the locked drawer of the chest. He patted his overcoat pockets and felt the shape of the two revolvers, one in each pocket. He should have left them in his office with the rest of the material evidence: the tube of red lipstick, the phial of poison, Aurigi's letter, the receipt from Garlini, the ticket stub from Aurigi's seat at La Scala.

But he had everything in his pockets.

Bah! Before long he would consign the items to the investigating magistrate and tell him to get on with it.

And the investigating magistrate would swiftly get on with having Aurigi arrested.

He sighed…

Cruni stood there watching him.

"Eh! My friend," murmured the inspector, just for the sake of saying something.

"The chief constable asked for you," Cruni offered timidly.

De Vincenzi shrugged his shoulders. He looked at the calendar. The same two red numbers he'd shown to Giannetto were still there, the ones that had forced him to admit to his losses on the stock exchange. In a strange association of thoughts, he again saw the Bank of Garlini, and the reddish, apoplectic cashier who'd held a packet of thousand-lire notes in his hand, saying: *I took it right in front of him… See? There was a hundred and now there's eighty… Do you want to count it?*

He jumped up. How could he have neglected that clue? He pulled his hat down and stood up straight, his eyes gleaming.

"Come with me," he ordered Cruni.

The sergeant quickly donned his overcoat and fetched his hat.

"Do you know where Garlini lives?"

"On via Leopardi."

"Hurry!"

Once outside the great door opening onto the piazza, he threw himself into a taxi. A colleague greeted him, but he didn't even see him.

"Via Leopardi!" he shouted to the driver.

Ten minutes later he and Cruni got out in front of Garlini's front door.

There he found an elderly housekeeper who began weeping and blowing her nose as soon as she saw him.

He began questioning her straightaway, without ceremony.

No, the signore had not returned home for supper the night before. No, she had not seen him since breakfast.

Where did he keep his money?

She pointed to a small safe.

Did he keep much of value in it? No, not much. Only what was necessary for housekeeping expenses.

De Vincenzi remembered that in his own pocket he had a small bunch of keys found in the dead man's pocket. The one to the safe was there, of course.

A simple safe, without a code.

He opened it and found nothing but envelopes, documents, a thousand or so lire and a few packets of letters from women bound with coloured string.

But Garlini had left the bank with twenty thousand lire in his pocket!

De Vincenzi appeared satisfied. He smiled and gave Cruni a friendly cuff on the shoulders. Cruni didn't understand a thing, in particular the reason for conducting such a search, without looking in any particular place and only glancing into the safe.

"Let's go now," De Vincenzi said.

When they got to the main door, he looked again at the time: it was almost three.

"We'll take the tram," he announced. "I want to arrive at three-thirty, and not before."

*

He entered Aurigi's apartment at half past three. He found the officer in the entrance hall.

"Anything new?"

"Nothing." The officer approached De Vincenzi to give an account of his time.

Aurigi had not eaten. He'd stayed in the drawing room, just where the inspector had left him.

"He hasn't even moved!" said the officer.

"And the other one?"

"In the kitchen or his room. He wanted to give me something to eat. He seems calm. In any case, he is certainly courteous."

"True," said De Vincenzi.

He went into the drawing room and greeted Giannetto, making a show of cheeriness.

"Beautiful day today! After all that fog last night, there's some sun."

With some irony, Aurigi replied, "That's natural. After the fog, there's always good weather."

He spoke just for the sake of it. He'd got up. He didn't even ask what De Vincenzi had done, or if he was sure he'd discover the killer. It was almost as if for him the crime had not taken place. As if nothing that had happened had anything to do with him.

De Vincenzi had left the door open, and now he saw Cruni bringing Count Marchionni and Maria Giovanna into the room.

The young woman was still dressed as she had been that morning. She looked at De Vincenzi with a bewildered air.

The count had regained his self-assurance: he was proud and correct, a proper gentleman paying a duty call. He bowed his head to the inspector.

"Here we are," he said, and he seemed to be asking him, as he might have an employee: What have you done? What do you intend to do?

In answer, De Vincenzi gestured for the count and his daughter to sit on the sofa.

"Have a seat, please."

He went to the drawing room door and called Cruni. He whispered a few words in his ear and the sergeant hurried to leave the room.

Then he ordered the other officer: "Go to the landing and close the door there. Wait for the investigating magistrate, and when he comes in, go down to the lodge with Cruni. The sergeant knows what to do."

The officer bowed his head. "Very well, sir." And off he went.

The entrance hall was now deserted. De Vincenzi glanced at the servant's room. The door was open, and he saw Giacomo reading next to the bed.

He closed the door to the drawing room. He drew from his pocket the revolver he'd taken from the servant and showed it to Aurigi.

"Do you recognize this revolver?"

Giannetto did not hesitate.

"It's mine. It should be in the drawer of that chest. I haven't touched it for years."

"Fine," said the inspector, and he put the revolver back in his pocket. He then took out the other one he'd found in the drawer.

"And this one?"

Aurigi's eyes widened. He had never seen that one before.

"This one," De Vincenzi said with some vigour, "is the revolver that killed Garlini. The ballistics expert has confirmed it."

He wrapped the gun in a handkerchief and put it on the table.

The others watched his actions. He paused for some time. Then, after a moment's hesitation, he made up his mind and went to the corner of the room, where he'd seen a bell.

After a spare few seconds, the door swung open and Giacomo appeared as if he'd been behind it, ready to be called.

The servant's smooth face was unruffled. But an attentive observer would have noted an odd gleam in his eyes, which could have been disguised apprehension as easily as curiosity.

De Vincenzi regarded him for a moment and then asked, "Would you bring me a glass of water?"

The servant bowed and went to the kitchen.

The inspector then headed for the door to the entrance hall and opened it, calling the officer from the landing.

"You—come here."

He ushered him into the dining room and showed him the revolver wrapped in the handkerchief.

"Take that revolver—but be very careful not to remove the handkerchief and not to touch it."

He stood near the table and spoke slowly. When the officer held out his hand to take the weapon, De Vincenzi made as if to stop him.

"Wait—I must tell you something else, give you some other instructions."

He was looking to gain time. Only when he heard Giacomo behind him did he turn suddenly. Cautiously, using only two fingers, he took the glass the waiter had brought him on a platter. He quickly emptied the water into a vase of flowers sitting on the table. He drew another handkerchief from the small pocket of his jacket, wrapped the glass in it and held it out to the officer.

"Take this." His voice had become hard.

"There are fingerprints on the revolver as well as the glass. Go to the Forensics Office right now and have them lifted. Quickly! I want the photographs within an hour."

The officer left rapidly with the two white handkerchiefs.

Giacomo had paled, but he displayed no obvious disturbance; rather a certain insolence, and a touch of sarcasm. He held his right hand out to De Vincenzi.

"Would you like my fingerprints?"

The inspector looked him over and took a sheet of white paper from his pocket.

"Let me see," he ordered sharply. He put the paper on the table.

With a wide grin, Giacomo extended his open hand and pressed the fleshy parts of his five fingers on the paper. He paused during the gesture, as if in challenge, and he stared at the inspector.

De Vincenzi watched him before asking, "What is your real name?"

The other man shrugged. "Giacomo Macchi."

"I will discover your real name before long. That's not it. You don't appear in any police files under that name and you are too experienced with fingerprints not to have a notorious past. How long have you been in this house?"

"I told you. Two years."

"Before that?"

The servant's insolence was pointed. "I brought references. If you want them, you can ask the signore." He gestured towards Aurigi, who was watching him.

"He was happy with me. I've never taken a thing from him in two years!"

The questioning was proceeding quickly. De Vincenzi obviously did not intend to let him off easily.

"And what time did you leave here last night?"

"Probably around ten... maybe before."

"The porter's wife didn't see you leave."

"But she can't say that she saw me leave later, either," Giacomo proclaimed triumphantly.

"Exactly! But after midnight the main door was closed."

"How can you say that I left after midnight?"

"There are people who saw you."

"Are you sure about that?" Giacomo asked sceptically.

De Vincenzi wagered everything he had. Either he'd get him to confess straightaway or—as he knew all too well—the man would never confess.

"The person who saw you will be here in a matter of minutes," he said confidently. "And he'll recognize you."

"I'll be happy to look that person in the face!"

The servant was clearly some way from feeling lost. After all, he must have found himself in similar situations before. He was too calm, too confident.

"You'll do so at four."

Giacomo turned to look at the clock. "So, another quarter of an hour to go."

The clock struck quarter to five, and De Vincenzi took Giacomo by the arm.

"That clock is showing four forty-five."

"I see that," Giacomo said. "But it's an hour fast."

"How do you know?"

This time the man seemed surprised.

"Eh?" he said, trying to gain time.

"I said," the inspector repeated, articulating every syllable, "I said, how do you know that the clock is running an hour fast?"

Giacomo paused for a second, but only a second.

"It's broken... I should have taken it to be fixed."

Aurigi intervened, his voice weary.

"That's not true, Giacomo. That clock was working just fine. It has always worked extremely well."

Giacomo flinched. Angry now, he turned towards his master.

"And now you too! Perhaps it was working well, but today it's not working properly."

An idea must have struck him. His eyes lit up and his confidence returned.

"As a matter of fact"—he turned to the inspector—"it was actually you who made a show in front of me that the clock was running fast."

It was true. De Vincenzi remembered it.

"True. And it's running fast because you put it forward last night."

"Me? Why would I have done that?"

"Why you did it, I shall tell you before long. It was a clever ploy, which immediately gave me the measure of your intelligence. A truly notable criminal intelligence! Yet none of this is extraordinary. The extraordinary thing is something else: that you didn't think to put the clock back after killing Garlini and before you left, and that you put the revolver used in the murder in the drawer—locking it and taking the key with you, as well as your master's revolver."

The servant listened. The smile remained on his lips.

"But what are you saying? Your imagination is running away with you. How are you going to prove all this?"

In fact, as De Vincenzi knew very well, he was using his intuition and this time, too, he had not a single piece of evidence. Yes, his intuition was telling him he'd hit the target, but how could he prove it? The man would never confess.

Nervous, he began pacing the room briskly. All at once he stopped in front of Giacomo.

"But you made a mistake. Everything was calculated, everything was ingeniously devised, and then it was all ruined by an oversight. If you'd put the hands back on the clock, I'd never have suspected you."

"And now?" Giacomo asked insolently.

"Now I know it was you who killed Garlini."

"Fantasy! I have an alibi. You can check it. And why would I have killed him? I barely knew him."

"His money?"

"What money? You think someone kills a man in order to rob him and then leaves five hundred lire in his pocket?"

The count had remained silent throughout, watching the scene with suppressed anxiety. At those words, he jumped up and advanced towards the servant.

Aurigi, too, sprang up.

But De Vincenzi made a move to hold them back and staved off their questions.

"How do you know," he asked, looking into Giacomo's eyes, "that Garlini had five hundred lire in his wallet?"

Giacomo looked lost for a moment. But while the others waited for him to keep quiet or offer some vague explanation, he broke into laughter. He took a newspaper from his pocket, unfolded it and left it open on the table.

"Read it. There, inside," he said calmly. "Read it and you'll see how anyone can find out that a wallet with five hundred lire in it and some calling cards was found on the body."

De Vincenzi was annoyed. The count, clenching his fists, returned to the sofa.

Giannetto fell back into his tragic apathy.

Maria Giovanna, who had heard nothing and seen nothing, continued to ponder her ruined life, her thwarted affections, and poor Remigio, whom she loved.

14

A Meeting with De Vincenzi

The man certainly knew how to defend himself.

But the irritation soon disappeared from De Vincenzi's face. Too clever! He'd given himself away.

"When did you read that newspaper?" asked the inspector, resuming his questioning.

"This morning."

"There weren't any newspapers here in the house. You could not have got hold of it while you were in there just now. Therefore, you had it with you, and you read it before coming here. Is that right?"

The servant did not understand. He asked plainly, "What if I did?"

"Oh, nothing," the inspector smiled briefly. "But let's be clear: you admit to having read that newspaper before coming in here two hours ago?"

"Of course. I told you so. I don't see how that can possibly matter."

"So why did you pretend not to know anything when I questioned you? Why did you come into this house as if nothing had happened? Why did you play the nonchalant who knows nothing and has a clean conscience?"

The questions came hammering out.

It was a blow for Giacomo. He went quiet. He looked around like a captive beast, his eyes flaming.

For the last time in that day full of dramatic events, the unconscious, innocent doorbell trilled long and loud.

Again, everyone jumped nervously.

De Vincenzi turned to the door almost angrily. Then he looked at Giacomo and his face lit up. He'd had an idea. He said to himself: It's the only way!

So he ordered the servant, "We'll take up this discussion later. Right now, though, go and open—"

Giacomo hesitated, as if realizing the inspector was setting a trap for him. He moved slightly, looked around once more and then started towards the entrance hall, in no hurry.

Marchionni clenched his fists and made as if to follow him.

"What are you doing? He's guilty! He'll escape!"

De Vincenzi stopped the count with a brusque gesture, almost nailing him to the spot with a look.

Meanwhile, Giacomo had opened the door and was standing aside in order to let in the investigating magistrate, followed by the court clerk.

The investigating magistrate came in quickly, smiling. He was a man of about thirty, with an ordinary face, a common aspect. The glasses sitting on his nose slid down every now and again, and he'd swiftly push them back into place with an automatic, almost tic-like movement.

As soon as he entered the room, he looked the three men in the face. He barely noticed Maria Giovanna, who had not risen from the sofa.

"The inspector?" he asked in turn.

De Vincenzi bowed.

"At your service, sir."

"Well? How have we got on? This seems a crime with a simple solution, am I right? And then of course," he added with irony, "you have some news, which you announced to me earlier."

Adjusting his glasses, he looked at the count and then at Maria Giovanna, who was getting up slowly, having shaken off her lethargy.

"These people?"

De Vincenzi introduced them. "Count Marchionni and his daughter."

"Witnesses?" asked the investigating magistrate, shaking the count's hand.

The inspector assumed a slight air of triumph.

"I believe we can do without them too."

"Ah," said the investigating magistrate, staring at him. Then, murmuring "Well, well," he made for the table and sat down, signalling for the clerk to sit down beside him.

The clerk took several sheets of paper from a leather case and spread them out on the table.

De Vincenzi moved so that he could watch the entrance hall. It was chiefly the door to the servant's room that attracted his attention. If his calculations were correct, the determining event should take place now. But he'd have to play for time while they waited.

So he spoke.

"A common crime, beautifully conceived and executed. The French call such crimes *crapuleux*, yet this one has particularly intelligent aspects. The goal was theft… the petty theft of money."

At these words, Marchionni and Giannetto, knowing that five hundred lire had been found in Garlini's wallet, expressed their astonishment.

De Vincenzi, with one eye still on the entrance hall, noticed their surprise and smiled.

"This morning, before I got here," he said, turning to Aurigi, "I, too, took a walk, and in Piazza Cordusio I stopped at the Garlini Bank. I questioned the employees and learnt that yesterday evening Garlini took twenty thousand lire from the safe and put the money in his pocket. Since I was able to establish that the money was not in his house, it's clear that he should have had it on him last night."

He turned again to the investigating magistrate.

"Being certain about this allowed me to exclude a motive of passion, and cleared the way for a petty one. Certainly, in principle anyone could have followed the trail of that receipt for half a million, and anyone could have committed an irreparable error. But if having left five hundred lire in Garlini's wallet was a stroke of genius that could derail the investigation from the beginning, it comes back to the general picture of premeditation, of clever and careful premeditation. Not only did the thief kill, but he did so by weaving such a firm web of evidence against other people that it would be impossible to suspect him—if the clock hadn't been there to sound the hours, and if I had not counted the strokes of the pendulum."

He pointed to the mantelpiece. The clock was striking four.

"Do you see, sir? Four—and it's actually three. Yesterday it struck eleven when it was ten... almost eleven."

He paused. The entrance hall was still empty. Would he be outsmarted? For a moment he feared Giacomo had left by another door, but told himself it was impossible. He'd seen every room of the apartment. As for the windows, no one would believe a man might leap some twenty metres.

"Sir, would you like the facts of the case, which will allow you to determine the accusation here and now, so that you can order the suspect's arrest and proceed to accuse him with peace of mind?"

"I ask for nothing else," said the investigating magistrate. He didn't know what to make of the inspector's wordiness.

"Here they are: a clock put forward by one hour; a revolver in a locked drawer; the spontaneous and unsolicited admission of the suspect that he heard a meeting taking place in this room yesterday afternoon; a phone call placed to the Duomo police station so that the murderer would be discovered as soon as possible, and in any case that night; and finally, some fingerprints, which may reveal a lot to us—but could also reveal nothing."

They're all just like him! the investigating magistrate thought to himself. Such pompous windbags. They're all so sure of themselves, these blessed inspectors. They investigate, discover things and never offer definite proof—and then the poor investigating magistrate is the one who gets into trouble.

"I see, I see," he murmured, settling his glasses on his nose. But he didn't see a thing.

"Good, good. But up to now, just clues. Expertly evaluated, but only clues. No confession! What if you're wrong, dear fellow? If you've gone down the wrong track, following an elaborate, juvenile fantasy, and you've lost sight of reality? It seems to me that the killer has—if we read the name written on this door and look at the bank balance, if we examine the life of the dead man and that of the suspected killer—how can I put this?—signed his own warrant!"

Giannetto was unperturbed. He knew all too well that the evidence was there, clear as day, to incriminate him. And he would truly have preferred to end the agony once and for all, for them to accuse and condemn him. He couldn't even consider taking up where he'd left off, now that he felt his spirit crushed and his heart in pieces.

"So right!" De Vincenzi replied to the investigating magistrate, tilting his head. He'd briefly been feeling less sure of himself. What he'd predicted had not happened. What if he really had been deceived? If all the clues were pointing to the servant, as they'd pointed to the others, were they actually pointing to an innocent, at the whim of chance?

The inspector knew all too well that he was risking his position and his career. That reedy little man with the glasses that wouldn't stay put had extremely set ideas. How could he convince him?

With his heart in his mouth, he looked at the hallway door, the door to the servant's room.

All at once his face lit up.

Giacomo had appeared at the door wearing his overcoat, hat in hand. He paused and looked around.

De Vincenzi quickly turned so that Giacomo would not notice that he'd been seen, and began talking again. He purposely raised his voice, making as much noise as possible to cover the killer's steps, which he alone could hear.

"So right! Everything you say is the theoretical explanation, I agree. The name on the door, the balance at the bank, the life of the dead man, above all the way the suspect had been living the past few months... so many facts, so much evidence. But you see, sir, sometimes facts deceive, and evidence lies. What does one need to be certain? Indeed—what does one need?"

He heard steps nearing the hallway door... he heard the door squeak slowly on its hinges... he detected the slight click of the lock springing shut.

He let out a sigh of relief and spoke quietly.

"But the reality is this, sir: that a killer never signs his own crime." He continued triumphantly. "No, sir, a killer never signs his own crime, although sometimes he signs his own confession. And our killer has confessed!"

The investigating magistrate jerked in such a way that this time his glasses fell to the table. His myopic eyes screwed up, he leant towards the inspector.

"Ah! He's confessed! Is that what you said? But a few moments ago, you were saying—"

"He had not confessed a few minutes ago! He is confessing this very instant with his escape."

"Escape?" the investigating magistrate shouted. He stood up. "But what are you saying?" He looked around, actually frightened. Not one of those in the room with him had moved.

"Who's escaping?"

Simply, as if he were pointing out the most natural and obvious thing, the inspector answered: "Giacomo Macchi, the servant. The killer."

The investigating magistrate looked at him, stupefied.

"But he's the one who opened the door to me. Or at least I thought it was he, since the man who opened the door had the air of a servant. How do you know he's escaped?"

"I saw him going—in this mirror."

De Vincenzi pointed to the mirror on the wall in which one could see the door in the entrance hall.

"Ah! By Jove! So you watched him leave and didn't even move? Why are you now waiting to have him followed?"

"I'm waiting till he's gone some way. For him to try to hide. For him to sign his confession clearly and conclusively. I had no other means of getting him to confess than giving him the chance to flee. He's a clever rascal, but he's fallen for the trap I prepared for him. He won't go far, you can be sure of it."

He looked at the investigating magistrate, who was unable to recover his earlier mood, and smiled before gently touching his arm.

"Sit down, sir, I'd ask you please to sit down again."

As if overpowered by De Vincenzi's calm assurance, the investigating magistrate sat. De Vincenzi stood in front of him and continued.

"So. Excellent. Now that I have your attention, I'll tell you how Giacomo Macchi killed Garlini."

He paused and avoided looking around, knowing that behind him were three souls in pain, and that even now his words could bring them no relief, because their tragedy was within, and not just that of a crime committed by someone else. He continued.

"What is a crime, sir, when it's not a crime of passion? It's a work of art! A work perversely and criminally artistic. And when I say a work of art, I mean that there's an element of fantasy, simple and concise in form, its constituent elements balanced, logical and coherent, clear and harmonious, vibrant and direct. So, nothing about the way this crime was conceived and executed could be considered more artistic… Listen to me, sir! Look at the background: a confusion of material and passionate interests means that at least two people want to kill a third. One of these two, reduced to extreme desperation, says to himself and perhaps to others: 'I'm clearly ruined—so I'll kill him' and makes an appointment with a third, the victim, in his own house, at midnight—that is, in this house, and for last night. That appointment and the desperate state of the person of whom we speak—we're talking here about Giannetto Aurigi, sir—are noted by his servant, Giacomo Macchi. That man is a criminal who's had many scores to settle with the law. He is sly, even genial. He knows his master has reached the point at which he might very well commit a crime, and he thinks he can prevent it, retaining every advantage for himself and ensuring that all suspicion falls on Aurigi. Are you following me, sir? So what does he do? He does this. He knows his master never carries a watch and, taking advantage of such knowledge—which may seem insignificant but is in fact crucial—he lies low after having set the clock in this room one hour ahead. He thinks: if Aurigi comes back first and looks at the clock, he'll tell himself he's missed the appointment, and Garlini won't be back. The killer leaves things to chance. And chance favours him, seeing to it that Aurigi goes out again, so the coast is clear. This is exactly what happened, sir. Do you understand now?"

Slowly and calmly, De Vincenzi continued to sketch his reconstruction of the crime.

EPILOGUE

About two months after the twenty-four hours that saw the unfolding of the tragic events just narrated, Inspector De Vincenzi, head of the flying squad at San Fedele, was in his office.

It was ten at night on Mardi Gras, and the carefree city spread itself out in front of San Fedele, through the streets, piazzas and public meeting places. The carnival period was proving markedly longer than in other years.

Shut up in his squalid room with the stained, cigar- and cigarette-burnt table, the worn-out armchairs, the shiny black telephone, De Vincenzi appeared to be reading a newspaper. Under a paper he kept spread out on the desk was an open book.

He was staring idly, a strange smile flickering across his face.

Once more he saw a neat room, sparsely furnished with some rather valuable antiques, coming off a corridor that led to the servants' quarters on the top floor. A young blond man with clear, loyal eyes, a wide, bright forehead, who invited him in with simple and unaffected courtesy.

Make yourself comfortable… I thought you would be back soon. And so? Have you found out?

The agitated youth had begun to sob loudly.

Poor young man, to be sure, thought De Vincenzi. His hours of anguish were over, but he'd experienced months, even years of pain. Finally, however, he was happy. That morning in March, actually on Mardi Gras, he'd married Maria Giovanna.

Actually, he—De Vincenzi—deserved a bit of credit for their happiness. Not only for having saved Maria Giovanna from being ruined by an ugly crime, and for lifting all suspicion from Giannetto Aurigi, but also because on the evening of the day he'd finished his conference with the investigating magistrate and had had the killer arrested—he'd not been able to get very far with his escape, followed as he was by Sergeant Cruni—De Vincenzi had had a long conversation with Count Marchionni.

A difficult conversation.

The elderly gentleman had known nothing about his daughter's love for Altieri. His wife had not dared reveal it to him. At first he'd flown off the handle, but he got through the awful ordeal, and his daughter with him, since for him to maintain an opposition that rigid would have brought nothing but more pain.

He'd given his consent, which for him meant renouncing all hope of a wealthy marriage for Maria Giovanna, and the dream of reconstructing his own fortunes with money from some hypothetical son-in-law.

He'd sold the palazzo, and after paying all his creditors, he had a little income left from some land in Comasco, and he'd retired there to live as a country gentleman with his wife and daughter.

Now Maria Giovanna was married.

Remigio Altieri had started working as an editor on a newspaper. The young man was clever, willing and respectable. He'd make his way.

They were happy.

They'd sent him a wedding invitation on white card, in the middle of which could be read only the names of the spouses. It was a simple wedding, almost secret, since the elderly count had dreamt of something quite other, and had not managed completely to renounce his dreams. Maria Giovanna had written in her own hand: *To our good friend and saviour in affectionate acknowledgement.*

The two were now set.

De Vincenzi smiled.

Every human drama, however terrible it may be, ends with signs of new life, with rebirth. Isn't it death, perhaps, which seeds life? Even the cypress is an evergreen.

Pondering all this, De Vincenzi dwelt almost obstinately on the memory of the two young people, imagining to himself their hard-won happiness, *seeing* them before him. He did not want to think about his childhood friend, the sad hero of the drama.

Giannetto Aurigi had closed up his apartment on via Monforte, sold all his furniture and gone away, leaving the apartment empty.

But where?

De Vincenzi didn't know, and it troubled him.

It had been a tough blow for Aurigi. The sort of pain that breaks one's heart irreparably and reveals a nasty, previously unknown side to human existence. It was all the worse for Giannetto since he had not himself been aware of just how deeply he loved his fiancée.

De Vincenzi had looked for him everywhere, and had had searches carried out. Perhaps he had gone abroad, who knows where, and De Vincenzi would have no further news.

Or maybe he'd see him in a few years. Changed: older, of course, but back to himself. He'd appear before him a little chubby, heavier, and he'd say with a smile, 'Who remembers that now, my friend! The world is as full as you like of all sorts of beautiful women, all of them ready for love.'

As long as he hadn't abandoned himself to a life of abject morals and degrading orgies with women…

Just then someone knocked on the door. De Vincenzi felt a twinge of impatience, but straightaway he thought: *this will help to distract me.*

With a movement he'd never forgotten, one that recalled the actions of students at the unexpected approach of their profs, he swept his book from the table into the drawer and said, "Come in!"

Giannetto Aurigi appeared in the doorway.

"Ah," said De Vincenzi, hardly able to believe his eyes, "you! And where have you been?" Giannetto's face was serious, but he seemed calm and serene.

He approached slowly, without answering. He put his hat and walking stick on a chair and sat down across from his friend, who'd got up to look him over.

"I've come to say goodbye, my friend. You know very well that I would never go away without saying something to you. I practically owe you my life! I'm leaving tomorrow."

"But you haven't already gone away?!" De Vincenzi asked with comic surprise. "Where have you been the last two months?"

"In Milan," Aurigi replied. "But I didn't want to see anyone. I've been through a miserable time. I could have disappeared for ever. I felt I'd gone out of my mind. My life had no meaning any more. I asked myself: why don't you end it all? So you can understand that with that sort of thing running through my head, I really had no desire to get out and about, to see friends or talk to anyone."

De Vincenzi listened.

Giannetto spoke in a calm voice. He was weighing up his words of desperation, reflecting on them. They seemed a long way from him, *and didn't belong to him any more*. It was apparent that he'd left that state of mind behind, and could describe it now precisely because it was no longer his.

"Well?" asked the inspector after a silence. "What now?"

"Oh," said Giannetto. He smiled. "It's over now. I'm leaving tomorrow. Know where I'm going?"

The other man shrugged.

"I'm going to Abyssinia. You'll remember that I'm a gunnery lieutenant—just like you, as it happens. We had our war together. Well, I proposed a return to active service in the colony, and I was welcomed. So I'll sail from Genoa tomorrow."

He stood up and held out his hand to De Vincenzi.

"Goodbye, my tried and trusted friend. I hope you won't have reason to regret having saved me from a bad situation."

They embraced.

When Giannetto was gone, De Vincenzi realized there were tears in his eyes.

——

▼ Did you know?

In 1929, when the Italian publisher Mondadori launched their popular series of crime and thriller titles (clad in the yellow jackets that would later give their name to the wider *giallo* tradition of Italian books and films) there were no Italian authors on the list. Many thought that Italy was inherently infertile ground for the thriller genre, with one critic claiming that a detective novel set in such a sleepy Mediterranean country was an "absurd hypothesis". Augusto De Angelis strongly disagreed. He saw crime fiction as the natural product of his fraught and violent times: "The detective novel is the fruit – the red, bloodied fruit of our age."

The question had a political significance too – the Marxist Antonio Gramsci was fascinated by the phenomenon of crime fiction, and saw in its unifying popularity a potential catalyst for revolutionary change. Benito Mussolini and his Fascist regime were also interested in the genre, although their attitude towards it was confused – on the one hand they approved of the triumph of the forces of order over degeneracy and chaos that most thriller plots involved; on the other hand they were wary of representations of their Italian homeland as anything less than a harmonious idyll.

This is the background against which Augusto De Angelis's *The Murdered Banker* appeared in 1935, the first of 20 novels starring Inspector De Vincenzi to be published over the next eight years. This period saw the peak of the British Golden Age puzzle mystery tradition, and the rise of the American hardboiled genre. However, De Angelis created a style all his own, with a detective who is more complex than the British "thinking machine" typified by Sherlock Holmes, but more sensitive than the tough-guy American private eye.

His originality won De Angelis great popularity, and a reputation as the father of the Italian mystery novel. Unfortunately, it also attracted the attention of the Fascist authorities, who censored De Angelis's work. After writing a number of anti-Fascist articles, De Angelis was finally arrested in 1943. Although he was released three months later, he was soon beaten up by a Fascist thug and died from his injuries in 1944.

So, where do you go from here?

If you want to follow De Vincenzi as he investigates a series of macabre murders in a seedy boarding house, track down De Angelis's gloriously Gothic *The Hotel of the Three Roses*.

If you fancy a real work-out for your little grey cells, take a look at Soji Shimada's legendary locked-room mystery, *The Tokyo Zodiac Murders*.

AVAILABLE AND COMING SOON
FROM PUSHKIN VERTIGO